JURYMEN MAY DINE

JURYMEN MAY DINE

Nick Boreham

Matador
Unit E2 Airfield Business Park,
Harrison Road, Market Harborough,
Leicestershire. LE16 7UL
Tel: 0116 2792299
Email: books@troubador.co.uk
Web: www.troubador.co.uk/matador
Twitter: @matadorbooks

ISBN 978 1805141 495

British Library Cataloguing in Publication Data.
A catalogue record for this book is available from the British Library.

Printed and bound in Great Britain by 4edge Limited
Typeset in 11.5pt Adobe Garamond Pro by Troubador Publishing Ltd, Leicester, UK

Matador is an imprint of Troubador Publishing Ltd

The hungry Judges soon the sentence sign,
And wretches hang that jury-men may dine

Alexander Pope

1

Flanked by prison officers, the defendant stood in the dock with his head bowed. It was probably only nervousness, but it made him look ashamed to show his face. The trial had been less than kind to that face. At the start it had been as fresh and trusting as a baby's. Now it was pinched and grey, as if its owner had spent years in prison already. He was dressed in a light blue suit and an open-necked shirt, he was twenty-nine years of age and his name was Conrad Connor.

I was the last to emerge into the full view of the court. I took my usual seat on the back row of the jury box, nearest the dock and furthest from the judge. The Honourable Mrs Justice Ede, eye-catching in her gaudy robes of red and black silk, was already sitting at her massive wooden bench high above us all. Behind her, the gigantic royal coat of arms lent an additional sense of theatre to the occasion, if one was needed. In her hand she held the slip of paper on which our verdict had been recorded. It was impossible to tell what she was thinking – her face, topped by the ridiculous horsehair wig, was as stony as ever. I was so tired and dismayed by the futile arguments and antiquated rituals of the last couple of weeks that I felt like walking out.

Down in the well of the court, the black-gowned barristers and pinstriped solicitors conversed in low tones, shuffled papers and threw searching stares at the jury. I'd been told that lawyers can predict the verdict from the way jurors behave when they return to court. If we think the defendant is guilty, we turn our eyes away from him. I looked at him.

A long time seemed to pass. The judge picked up her pen and wrote with it. There was a minor disturbance in the public gallery, followed by an urgent shushing and scraping of shoes on bare boards. If they'd wanted to prolong the defendant's agony, this was a good way of going about it. But at last Mrs Justice Ede put down her pen, the clerk of the court rose to his feet and an expectant hush fell on the varnished wooden benches. Conrad Connor, the loneliest man in the world at that moment, kept his eyes on the floor.

'Will the foreman please stand?'

Stan Tuffin was sitting in the front row of the jury box. He stood up obediently, clutching his notebook to his chest.

'Please answer yes or no to the question I put to you,' the clerk intoned. 'Has the jury reached a verdict on which at least ten of you are agreed?'

'Yes.'

'On the count of murder, do you find the defendant Conrad Connor guilty or not guilty?'

There was a long silence. As the court waited for his reply, my opinion of Stan Tuffin sank even lower. He didn't seem to understand the question.

'For God's sake, out with it,' the juror beside me muttered under her breath.

The clerk put the question again.

Stan looked round apprehensively, as if he was the one on trial, then in a far-from-confident voice said, 'Guilty.'

For a split second nothing happened. Then everything did. The defendant clutched at the dock as if someone had shoved him from behind. A woman screamed. A man shouted, 'He didn't do it — ask Miss Prim.' Apart from that, the verdict was a popular one. A sustained burst of clapping and cheering from the public gallery soon drowned out the defendant's few supporters.

'Silence!' shouted the clerk. The judge glowered as if she was going to pass sentence on the public as well as on the defendant.

'Is that the verdict of you all, or a majority?'

'A majority.' Stan's voice had faded to a whisper.

'How many agreed?'

There was another pause. The judge waited. Stan opened his notebook as if to remind himself, then snapped it shut. I got the impression he was attempting a mental head count.

'Eleven,' he said.

'How many dissented?'

'One.'

I looked at the defendant again but he had disappeared from view. The officers hauled him off the floor, sat him on a chair and clamped their hands on his shoulders.

Mrs Justice Ede glared at him with undisguised contempt, then spoke in a voice that chilled the air. 'Stand up.'

The officers pulled him to his feet.

'Conrad Connor,' she said, 'you have been convicted of a cowardly and despicable crime. I have no doubt whatsoever that the jury have returned the correct verdict.

'For some time, you had been sharing a flat with a talented young artist, Douglas Hamilton. Earlier this year, on the morning of Saturday the sixth of February, you killed him with a single shot to the chest. There is no doubt in my mind that your motive was jealousy of your flatmate's success. I have heard convincing evidence of this.

'As Douglas's body lay bleeding at your feet, you fled in panic and went to the railway station, where you boarded a train. Your intention was to provide yourself with an alibi. But you were not careful enough. You left three live cartridges in the top drawer of your bedside cabinet, cartridges which fitted the gun that ended Douglas's blameless life. The weapon itself was discovered when the police conducted a search of the back yard. Your defence that you were on the train when the murder was committed is spurious. I am convinced that it was possible for you to kill Douglas, conceal the gun and get to the station in good time to catch your train.

'Conrad Connor, your actions were evil beyond

imagination. Douglas Hamilton was a well-liked young man who was building a fine reputation as an artist, a profession for which both of you had trained. He was beginning a new stage in his career. Success beckoned, the fruit of his undoubted ability and hard work. But you, Conrad Connor, cut him down on the threshold of the recognition he so richly deserved. It was a wicked, senseless act that deserves the highest penalty.

'In passing the mandatory sentence for the crime of murder, I have to consider when it will be safe for you to be released from prison. I find it difficult to believe that it will ever be safe to release a man such as you. Nonetheless, Conrad Connor, I pass on you the sentence of imprisonment for life on the count of murder, and recommend that you serve a minimum of thirty years.'

And that was that. I watched as Conrad was half-led, half-carried through a door at the back of the court to a dark place from which he could not expect to return for decades. The court was called upon to stand as the judge made her stately exit. Then we, the men and women of the jury, were free to go. A court official gave us back our mobile phones and handed us our claim forms. All such business done, we filed out of the courtroom, avoiding each other's eyes and the stares of the onlookers.

I headed straight for the gents. A couple of young men I'd noticed in the public gallery were standing in adjacent stalls, excitedly discussing the verdict. I chose a stall as far away from them as possible, but I could not avoid hearing what they said. They were friends of the victim, it seemed.

'Held the gun close, the firearms expert said.'

'That's why there were burn marks on his skin.'

'Bat-shit crazy.'

'And all he got was thirty years. He'll be out again in fifteen.'

'No, he got life. Thirty's the tariff. That means he has to do thirty before they consider him for parole. Might not get it even then. Could be inside for ever.'

'Should have hung him. Would've been cheaper.'

Outside the court, the narrow street was packed with reporters, photographers and a restless crowd of spectators. The air of celebration disgusted me. Jubilant police officers were gathering on the courthouse steps, shaking hands with each other as if they'd won a major sporting competition. In their midst Theresa Hamilton, the murdered man's mother, a tall and strikingly beautiful woman whose testimony had been so damaging to the defendant, stood in front of a microphone. She waited for a technician to adjust it, then read out a statement on behalf of the family.

'Douglas was our only son,' her voice crackled from the speakers. 'All we have left of him is memories, wonderful memories which we will keep in our hearts for ever. We have suffered a devastating loss – Douggie was our best friend as well as our hope and joy. Our lives have changed for ever. But the family's pain is lessened by the knowledge that justice has been done. We will leave others to pass moral judgement on the twisted individual who took Douglas from us. As his family, we will limit ourselves to expressing our gratitude to the police for their determination to see the case through. And to thanking the jury for their courageous decision.'

I could have laughed out loud. Our courageous decision? It was supposed to be beyond reasonable doubt, but there were more doubts in this case than hairs in Mrs Justice Ede's wig. In the all-too-short period we spent in the jury room, I'd pointed out weakness after weakness in the prosecution case. I'd begged my fellow jurors to consider what it could do to Conrad if we made a hasty decision. But they'd ignored me and returned a majority verdict of guilty in record time.

If I'd had the guts to grab the microphone from Mrs Hamilton and tell the world there was another side to the case, something that had not been mentioned in court, things might have turned out differently. But I pushed my way through the crowd and set off for my hotel.

'Sir – excuse me, sir – please—'

Turning to see who was yelling, I spotted a young woman racing after me. She was short and slim, not much more than five feet tall. Strands of blonde hair blew across her face as she ran. The way she hunched her shoulders gave the impression she was running for her life.

'You were at the trial,' she said, brushing the hair away as she arrived breathless at my side. She wore a long navy coat with a red beret. She was pretty but her cheeks were unnaturally pale, like a full moon on a cold winter night. It made her dark grey lipstick stand out all the more.

'You were on the jury, weren't you?' she said. It was more of an accusation than a question.

We'd been warned not to tell anyone how we came to our decision. Not even our families, and certainly not the press. At first, I thought she was a reporter after a cheap story.

'What if I was?' I said.

'And you were the one?' She grabbed my arm. This is no reporter, I said to myself. She's too upset for that.

'I'm sorry, I don't understand,' I said. 'What do you mean, "the one"?'

'The one who wanted to acquit Conrad.'

A gust of chilly September wind blew down the street, lifting the hem of her coat and wafting more strands of hair across her face. This time she didn't bother to brush them away. She moved closer to me, as if she needed my protection.

'What makes you think I wanted to acquit him?' I said.

'I saw the look on your face when the foreman said "guilty". Then, when I heard that the jury was divided eleven-to-one, I was sure of it.'

'I was the one, yes. But the other eleven didn't agree with me. They were convinced of his guilt. Right or wrong, that's all that matters. It's the way the system works.'

'But he's innocent.'

If she hadn't looked so miserable, I would have turned my back on her. No one could have known whether Conrad Connor was innocent or guilty. The case was wreathed in uncertainty. There was a great deal of evidence against him, but it was all circumstantial. To my mind, that left plenty of room for doubt. It was what we'd argued about in the jury room. I'd said there wasn't enough to convict him, the others had said there was.

'What makes you think he's innocent?' I said.

The young woman's eyes filled with tears. 'Because I'm his sister.'

My stomach clenched. I was one of the twelve men and women who'd locked Conrad Connor in a concrete box for the greater part of his life, if not for ever. It wasn't easy to look his sister in the face.

'I'm sorry,' I said. 'It must have been difficult, watching your brother...' I didn't finish. Everything was coming back to me. The look of incomprehension on Conrad's face when the judge pronounced sentence, quickly becoming fear. The way he chewed his lower lip. That other vicious sentencing, all those years ago.

By now the young woman was sobbing. It was embarrassing. Passers-by stared at me as if I'd done something bad to her. 'Come on,' I said. 'I'll buy you a coffee. You need to sit down.'

We found a café a few yards along the road. A couple of students were staring at computer screens over empty cups, but there were plenty of quiet corners to choose from. I led my sniffling companion to a secluded alcove, bought us drinks and sat down beside her.

'My name's Tony Quirke,' I said, for want of something to say.

She dabbed her eyes with a tissue. 'Janet Connor.'

After that, neither of us spoke. I didn't want to start a

conversation because I didn't want to upset her again. The thoughts that filled my head would only have troubled her. They were best left unsaid. I looked out at the darkening sky and the rain that was beginning to streak the window panes. Fitting weather for a depressing day. I sipped my coffee, wondering how I could leave her without seeming rude.

She was the first to break the silence. In a distant voice she said, 'I don't know how anyone could do it.'

I assumed she meant convict her brother.

'That's how I feel too,' I said. I didn't want her to think I'd played a part in it. 'When it became obvious that we were never going to agree, the judge decided she'd accept a majority verdict. From then on, it was hopeless. I argued and argued, but I only had one vote out of twelve. In the end, it counted for nothing.'

Janet's eyes flashed with anger. 'I'm not quite sure what you're saying.'

I was beginning to regret having anything to do with her. 'Your brother didn't have a chance against the prosecution barrister,' I said. 'Ursula Jolliffe had him on a skewer. She even made him look guilty.'

'What do you mean, look guilty?'

'Were you in court when Jolliffe asked him outright, "Conrad Connor, did you kill Douglas Hamilton?"'

'I was there for the whole trial.'

Yes, she had been. I remembered her now. She'd been sitting in the front row of the public gallery.

'So you'll know how your brother reacted,' I said. 'He didn't answer the question. He stood there shifting from foot to foot in total silence. He couldn't even lift his eyes off the floor. It made him look guilty. And it turned the rest of the jury against him.'

'It's what he's like,' Janet said, tears filling her eyes again. 'He's shy. He's an artist. He's not used to talking in public. If you say anything challenging, he vanishes into his shell and hopes you'll go away.'

'I did my best for him,' I said. 'I feel for you, Janet, I do. But there's always the chance of an appeal. You ought to be talking to his lawyers, not to me. I'm out of it now.'

She sniffed.

I emptied my cup. Yes, I was angry too. When a man can lose everything because he rubs the jury up the wrong way, even when there's no hard evidence against him, the system isn't faulty, it's corrupt. Conrad Connor wasn't the first and he wouldn't be the last – no one could know that better than me.

I was about to wish Janet good luck with the appeal and take my leave when she came out with it. The remark that set the whole thing going.

'Conrad would never use a gun,' she said. 'It's not like him. Someone else did it, Mr Quirke. And I know who it was.'

When you've spent two weeks trying to decide whether a man is innocent or guilty of murder, then a stranger tells you they've known all along that someone else did it, you prick up your ears and listen.

'What do you mean, you know who it was?'

'Oh, I don't know his name.' Janet tossed her head. 'But Doug Hamilton was into drugs. He'd got to know the candy men. I think he owed them money, and when he didn't pay up, they did what monsters like that do.'

She started crying again. Without thinking, I took hold of her hand. Instead of pulling it away, she gripped me tight. We sat there in silence, aware of the bond that was growing between us.

'Will you do something for me?' she said.

I waited.

'Will you help me get my brother's sentence overturned?'

I felt a cold sweat coming on. Challenge a legal decision? I tried to pull my hand away but she wouldn't let me.

'I don't think I could,' I said. 'If you're sure a drug dealer did it, why don't you go to the police?'

'You don't know the police like I do.'

'I'm sorry, I can't.'

She reddened. 'You could speak out,' she said. 'Tell them what you just told me. That the jury were swayed by – by what you said. By things that didn't count, by the way Conrad looked in the dock—'

I shook my head.

She let go of my hand. 'You keep saying you're sorry, but I'm the one who should be sorry. When I saw you in that jury box I thought, "He's a man with a heart." I saw your face when that revolting lawyer was dragging Conrad's name through the mud. I thought that you were on Conrad's side. How wrong I was. You're as bad as the rest of them.'

'Don't say that, Janet. It's not that I don't want to

help. I don't have the knowledge or the skills. You need a lawyer, not someone like me.'

She brought out a scrap of paper. 'Have you got a pen?'

I searched my pockets and found one.

She scribbled something down.

'My number,' she said. 'If you change your mind, give me a call.' She squeezed my hand. 'Don't let me down, Mr Quirke, please.'

2

I'd been staying in a budget hotel not far from the Crown Court. After saying goodbye to Janet, I hurried through the rain-soaked back streets of the unfamiliar Essex town trying not to think about the trial. There were better things to occupy my mind. As soon as I was back in my hotel room, I got out my phone and started planning my holiday.

Or tried to. I'd had every intention of putting jury service behind me, and certainly no desire to challenge the conviction. But after meeting the convicted man's sister, it was impossible to get Conrad Connor out of my mind. As I'd told Janet, it was an unequal contest between Conrad and the prosecution barrister, Ursula Jolliffe KC. A woman with a brilliant forensic mind, some would say, but I preferred to call it sadistic. Once she got to work, Conrad was finished.

She went into the attack from the start, when the judge called on the prosecution to open the case for the Crown. Jolliffe rose to her feet, looking remarkably like a Halloween witch in full regalia. Turning to address the jury, she gave us a charming smile. 'I will begin by summarising the evidence I will present throughout the trial,' she said.

She made it sound so believable. Conrad Connor and Douglas Hamilton had met at a college on the outskirts of London. They'd been studying art, and like most fledgling artists, struggled financially at the end of their course. After they moved into a flat together, Conrad had given up painting completely. He'd found a part-time job in a supermarket, and worked his shifts while Doug toiled at his easel.

Toil that had paid off, Jolliffe told us. In the autumn preceding the murder, Doug had been discovered by the Willoughby Gallery, a fine art business in the East End of London. Sitting in that overheated courtroom, the jury listened spellbound as Jolliffe described how well Doug had been doing. She then put the same amount of effort into telling us what a waste of space Conrad had been. He didn't even do his share of the housework. Doug had to cook their meals and do their washing. All Conrad did when he wasn't working at the supermarket, according to Jolliffe, was lie on his bed and play games on his computer.

Because of Doug's success, a tension had developed between the two young men that hadn't existed before. We would hear evidence, Jolliffe promised us, that

Conrad was so full of jealousy that he had row after row with Doug, most of which focused on Doug's relationship with the director of the Willoughby Gallery. This was a character called David Platinga, a much older man who got Doug favourable mentions in art magazines and took him to smart parties. Before long, Doug was mingling with the great and the good of the art world, and Conrad was feeling left out.

A few weeks before the murder, Doug had told Conrad he was thinking of moving closer to London. He wanted to be within easy reach of the Willoughby, now the focus of his entire existence. According to Jolliffe, Conrad had reacted to this suggestion with fury. His resentment increased, so we were told, until he decided to end Doug's life. If he couldn't have Doug for himself, David Platinga wasn't going to have him either. Somehow Conrad acquired a handgun, and early on the morning of Saturday the sixth of February, as the crisis in their relationship came to a head, he held the gun to Doug's chest and pulled the trigger.

Janet must have gone through agonies hearing it dragged out in open court. I could understand why she was angry, but what she wanted from me wasn't feasible. I looked round my poky hotel room and felt an overpowering urge to get away. Away from everything – murder trials, grieving relatives, the never-ending rain. My holiday starts here, I said to myself. I had a month of annual leave due – my boss had allowed me to postpone it until I'd finished jury service. The evening lay before me, I was thirsty and the hotel bar was as inviting as a dentist's waiting room. I didn't know anybody in the locality, so I abandoned the idea of spending the night on the town. If I was going to drink alone, I might as well do it in my hotel room. Then tomorrow I'd book my tickets.

I was woken from a dream about sunny Italy by my phone ringing. It was eight o'clock in the evening and already dark. The cans I'd brought back to the hotel were finished, my head was fuzzy and my neck was stiff from falling asleep in the armchair.

The caller was an old friend, Phil Gilland.

'Tony? Is that you?'

'Phil! Where have you been all this time, you old goat?'

'In the States – Hollywood, no less. Just got back. I'll fill you in later.' He paused. 'I hope you don't mind me phoning. I dropped by your bungalow but you weren't at home.' Another pause. 'Clarissa told me your news.' He sounded embarrassed.

'That's all right,' I said. 'Don't bother yourself. We finally decided to end it. It's perfectly amicable, no hard feelings at all.' Liar, I said to myself.

'She said you'd moved into a hotel.'

'Just for now.' My room was stacked with bin bags full of clothes, my wetsuit and paddle board, my laptop and anything else I could cram into my Volvo. Clarissa had given me half an hour to move out.

'Where are you now?' I said.

'A hundred yards down the lane from your bungalow,

parked on the verge. I should have rung before I turned up. Sorry about that. Didn't think. Stupid of me.'

'Time for a beer?'

'I can come to your hotel, if you tell me where it is.'

Phil Gilland had made a career for himself as a screenwriter, specialising in crime. He wrote dialogue for video games too. If Clarissa wasn't prepared to tell him which hotel I was staying at, she must have given him a hard time when he appeared on the doorstep. She had an unfortunate habit of tarring my friends with the same brush as myself. But I wasn't going to apologise on her behalf. I told Phil the name of the hotel and we agreed to meet in the lobby.

'Good to catch up with you, you young rascal!' he yelled as he burst through the swing doors, as full of bounce as ever. He looked plumper than when I'd seen him last, about a year and a half earlier. His hair, which he wore in a thick fringe about an inch above his eyebrows, seemed lighter than I remembered. He was forty, nearly ten years older than me, but too young to be going grey. Maybe his hair had bleached in the Californian sun. He'd certainly got a fine tan.

Plonking his six-foot, rugby-playing frame into the armchair next to mine, he looked round the tatty hotel lobby with a frown, then grinned.

'Nice place you've got here.'

'I'll be moving on before long,' I said. 'Where to, I've no idea, but this'll do for the time being.'

'So what have you been up to?'

I'd been leafing through the evening paper while I

waited for him. There was a picture of Conrad Connor on the front page, one that made him look even more shifty than he'd looked in the dock. It must have been a police mugshot. *Killed Flatmate for Spite*, the headline trumpeted. Phil's eyes went straight to it. 'The Hamilton murder case?' he said, raising his eyebrows.

'I was on the jury,' I said.

'Were you now?' Phil sounded impressed. He'd been following the case while he was in the States, he told me. I suppose crime writers need to keep abreast of these things. It's their stock-in-trade. He took the evening paper off me and studied the front page. 'Majority verdict,' he mused. 'Wonder how it came to that. Seemed an open-and-shut case to me.'

'Where are we going to drink this evening?' I said, ignoring his attempt to prise a story out of me. It was a long time since I'd had a bladderful with a mate.

We drove in Phil's car to a centuries-old hostelry with low ceilings and exposed beams. It was the sort of pub I like. There were no other customers apart from a couple of old men playing dominoes, and no more noise than the slow ticking of the railway clock over the bar. We drank real ale while Phil told me about the script conference he'd been attending. After that, we talked about rugby. But I suppose it was inevitable that we would end up discussing the trial.

'It was well reported,' Phil said. 'I can't see room for the slightest scintilla of doubt. Connor did a runner on the morning of the murder, didn't he? To – where was it?'

'Colchester.'

'That's right. A desperate attempt to prove he wasn't in the flat when his flatmate was killed. What more evidence do you want than that?'

'He was visiting a friend,' I protested.

'And what about the spare cartridges? Murderers have gone to the gallows for less.'

'Doesn't prove a thing.'

Phil looked at me as if I'd taken leave of my senses.

'It's not enough to connect him to the crime,' I said.

'Not enough to connect him? The cartridges were in the top drawer of his bedside cabinet. That connects him.'

'You can't assume he put them there.'

Phil guffawed. 'That's ridiculous. He lost his nerve after shooting his flatmate, that's why he forgot about the cartridges. He was so desperate to get to the station that he stopped thinking straight.' Phil was beginning to sound shirty. That's the one thing I've got against him. He doesn't like losing an argument.

'Eleven-to-one,' he said. 'Tell me, who was the oddball on the jury who couldn't see what was staring them in the face? Who was the bleeding heart who wanted to let Connor off?'

'You know I can't talk about it,' I said. 'Jury deliberations are supposed to be secret.'

'No need to tell me,' he said. 'I'm getting a picture of her already.' He leaned back in his chair, stretched out his legs, closed his eyes and moved his hands in the air. It made him look like a medium calling up a spirit from the underworld. 'In her eighties,' he said. 'Single. Puts out food for the birds in winter. Often seen at rail stations rattling a collecting tin.'

'Come off it, Phil. Another pint?'

He sat bolt upright. 'Bloody hell. It was you, wasn't it?'

'You make it sound like a crime, Phil.'

'Letting a killer off is most definitely a crime.' He looked shocked.

'All you know is what was reported in the media,' I said. Janet Connor's words about the murdered man were ringing in my ears. *He'd got to know the candy men. I think he owed them money, and when he didn't pay up, they did what monsters like that do.* 'Sure, the police found cartridges in the flat. But maybe someone called on Doug after Conrad left for Colchester. Maybe this unknown person had an issue with Doug. An argument flared up, this other person shot him, planted evidence to incriminate Conrad and ran for it. To my mind, that's a believable scenario. It might not have happened, of course. But as long as it hasn't been excluded, there's reasonable doubt. And reasonable doubt means not guilty.'

'But the cartridges had Connor's DNA on them,' Phil said. 'That's what convinced me.'

'Don't jump to conclusions. They swabbed Conrad for gunshot residue and found nothing. Not on his skin, not on his clothes. It's true, they found his DNA on the cartridges, but not his fingerprints. Didn't you ever wonder why?'

Phil frowned. 'I don't remember reading anything about fingerprints.'

21

'The flat was a tip,' I said. 'There were used tissues everywhere, dirty underwear on the beds and God knows what. The killer could have contaminated the cartridges with Conrad's DNA. He couldn't put Conrad's prints on them, but he only had to wipe them with a tissue from under Conrad's pillow and Conrad was in the frame. The DNA doesn't prove a thing.'

Phil laughed. 'You're not going to give up, are you? But you haven't made me change my mind. If I'd been on that jury, the decision would have been unanimous.'

'There's no use arguing,' I said. 'It's over now. Done and dusted.'

Phil thought for a while. 'Maybe it isn't.'

'It is for me,' I said. 'This is where I'll be next week.' I got out my phone and showed him some of the websites I'd been looking at. *Autumn Vacations in Italy – Italian City Breaks – Best of Venice (Eight Days Tour).* 'My holiday started the moment my jury service came to an end. That was hours ago, so I'm wasting time already. Remember Marion?'

Phil shook his head.

'One of those teachers we knew in Earl's Court?'

'Oh yes, the one you fancied. The one who went to Viareggio and married a count.'

'A film director,' I said. 'I heard they'd separated. Marion's living on her own in Venice, so I thought I'd look her up.'

I showed Phil a shot of the Grand Canal.

'No, listen,' he said. 'Light bulb moment. You've got one hell of an angle on this case, Tony.'

'So?'

'If you gave me the inside story, clashes in the jury room, jurors arguing about the evidence, stuff like that, I reckon I could get an episode out of it.'

'An episode?'

'I don't think I told you. I'm doing a crime series for a TV company. We start shooting in less than two weeks. But there's still scripts to be written – this could be a great opportunity for both of us.'

'I don't follow you,' I said.

Phil was so excited he was jogging the table. 'The way you're trying to turn the prosecution case on its head – I like it. And you were in the thick of it, slap-bang in the centre of the action. It's good material. I can see a plot in it. No, two plots. Two whole episodes. Factor in a bent juror—'

'No, Phil.'

'We'll share the fee. Fifty-fifty.'

'How many times have I got to say no?'

'Sixty-forty.'

I shook my head. 'Sorry, but I'm on holiday from now on.'

Phil threw himself back in his chair, angry because he'd lost a story. His interest in the case had evaporated. 'Oh well,' he said, 'I suppose you know your own mind. Sorry I leaned on you.'

3

Next morning I woke with a hangover, pulled back the curtains and looked out at another overcast sky. Judging by the tops of the trees, a stiff breeze was getting up. More rain would be blowing in soon – a good day to buy a ticket for Italy. I decided to put my belongings into storage, book a flight to Venice and check out of the hotel. I could find somewhere permanent to live when I got back.

Opening my door, I removed the *Do Not Disturb* sign, picked up the morning paper and stood in the corridor skimming the headlines. The defence secretary had delivered a speech on diversity in the armed forces. A high court judge had been arrested for clubbing a fox to death. Then, tucked away at the bottom—

MURDERER KILLS HIMSELF IN CELL

The article was on an inside page. I went straight to it.

Newly convicted killer Conrad Connor has committed suicide, hours after being sentenced to life in prison for his bloody crime.

He'd done it in the holding cell at the Crown Court. There was supposed to be a suicide watch, but he'd managed to hang himself before the transfer van arrived, using his shirt sleeve for a noose. Weren't they supposed to check him every half hour?

A door opened further down the corridor and a couple came out of their room pulling suitcases. They gave me a funny look as they walked past. Realising that I was standing there in my boxers, I dropped the paper and went back into my room. The sound of the door closing behind me was like a cell door slamming shut. It made me think of my father, convicted fifteen years earlier because the jury had believed the lies of a resentful school kid. Something that was never corroborated. Something that was never proved.

More than anyone, I knew what the news would have done to Janet. She'd asked for my help. Any decent person would have said, 'Yes, I'm with you all the way, I know about the case, I'll do all I can to get him off.' But I'd let her down. If Conrad had known there was someone on his side, a member of the jury no less, someone willing to help him with an appeal—

I reached for my phone. Should I? Shouldn't I?

I did. I phoned the number Janet had scribbled down. There was no answer, so I left a message.

'Janet, this is Tony Quirke. Remember me? We spoke after the trial. I'm the juror who didn't agree with the verdict. I'm phoning because I've just heard the news. I want to tell you how shocked I am. I don't know what to say. But if you'd like to talk, feel free to give me a call.'

After that, I got dressed and went downstairs in search of black coffee. That gave me my second shock of the morning. Waiting for me at reception I found an official-looking envelope. I tore it open and discovered that it was from Clarissa's solicitors. By way of a settlement, she was demanding the bungalow and the whole of my pension. A fog of bitterness descended. We'd agreed not to go to lawyers. I'd thought we'd made a clean break but obviously we hadn't. She was trying to cut me off at the knees. If I wanted to fight her, I'd need a solicitor of my own, a good one. And that sort of solicitor didn't come cheap.

Phil was only too glad to meet up again. He arrived at the hotel just before lunch.

'What made you change your mind?' he said.

'The money. But I'm insisting on a slight modification to your proposal.'

'Oh yes?'

'I don't want to work on your TV series. I want us to collaborate on a true crime book about the Hamilton case. It got a lot of publicity, so there's bound to be a market for it.'

Phil scratched his chin. 'I've never written true crime.'

'But you're a crime writer.'

He pulled a face. 'I suppose so.'

'I want to question the safety of the conviction,' I said. 'British justice blunders again.'

'Right,' said Phil, with a slight inflection of his voice that meant, 'I'm not so sure.'

'I want to show how fallible the criminal justice system can be,' I said. 'It was the same old monkey business – a prosecution that went to work on the jurors' prejudices. Conrad was convicted by lawyers' trickery, not by evidence.'

'Could it be made to stick?'

'Don't worry, I'll make it stick.'

'I suppose we could have some powerful courtroom dramas,' Phil conceded.

'I can't reveal what happened in the jury room,' I said, 'but no one knows the details of the case better than me.' I paused to let that sink in, then said, 'And I've got a great source – Conrad's sister Janet. She'll have a lot to tell us, you can bet your entire TV series on that.'

Phil looked impressed. 'How come you know the convicted man's sister?'

I told him how Janet had run after me at the end of the trial. I told him her theory that Doug Hamilton had been killed by a drug dealer, and how keen she was to have the case reopened.

'Well…' said Phil. He still sounded doubtful but I could tell he was hooked. 'A true crime book along those lines might just sell. I'll have to speak to my agent. Where did you say it happened?'

'A little place called Riverwell,' I said, 'on the north

bank of the Thames estuary. Not far from the container port.'

'Oh yes,' said Phil, 'I've heard of it. Just off the A13, isn't it?'

'The A13 runs north of it. The murder happened in a rundown street called Johnson Terrace. Doug Hamilton and Conrad Connor shared a room in number 14.'

'The Thames estuary,' said Phil, 'not far from the container port. A stomping ground for dealers, thieves and con men. Half the country's cocaine comes in through that port. We thought about shooting the TV series there, although we went to Newcastle in the end. According to our researcher, you're more likely to be robbed, stabbed or shot around there than anywhere else in England. And things are getting worse, they say. I like it. Mists rolling in from the sea, foghorns echoing along the muddy foreshore, a horrible murder. It's Dickensian. I like it a lot.'

'Look here,' he said after we'd ordered our meals in the little restaurant we went to for lunch, 'if we want to question the verdict, we've got one hell of a mountain to climb. I hear what you say about the DNA and so forth. But from what I read in the media, the prosecution blew Conrad's Colchester alibi out of the water. He said he was on the train when his flatmate was killed, didn't he? But the prosecution proved he wasn't. In most people's eyes, that means he was guilty.'

I hoped Phil wasn't having second thoughts. 'I have

to admit that Conrad's movements on the morning of the murder were a problem for the defence,' I said. 'But don't get it out of proportion.'

Phil shook his head. 'If I'm going to persuade my agent to take us on, I'll need to convince her that the prosecution got it wrong.'

'There's no doubt Conrad went to the station and caught the eight forty to Fenchurch Street,' I said, 'after which he walked to Liverpool Street and caught the train to Colchester. We can't challenge that. CCTV footage showed him at all four stations, and the eight forty ran on time.'

Our meals arrived.

'So what can we challenge?' Phil said after the waitress had gone.

'We can challenge the time Doug was shot,' I said. 'According to the prosecution, Conrad killed him at ten past eight. That gave Conrad plenty of time to catch the eight forty. The station's only a few minutes away. But maybe Doug wasn't shot at ten past eight. Maybe he was shot later than that. Maybe he was shot after Conrad's train had departed.'

'So what do I say to my agent?' Phil asked, spearing a gnocchetti with his fork.

'Tell her the time Doug died was never conclusively established,' I said. 'There was only one witness – a librarian called Mrs Glynis Wilderman. She was walking her dog along Johnson Terrace when she heard a gun go off. She swore that the noise came from inside Doug and Conrad's flat, and that she heard it at ten past eight. Tell your agent we're going to cast doubt on the accuracy of Mrs Wilderman's testimony. It was never corroborated. So how do we know she wasn't mistaken? As long as there's room for doubt, the conviction remains unsafe.'

Phil put down his fork, an amused expression on his face. 'It's going to take a lot of hard work to prove she got the time wrong. Librarians are usually pretty good at watching the clock. How are you placed over the next few months?'

'I'm on my annual leave,' I reminded him. 'After that I'm back at work.'

'So what can you do while you're on leave?'

Up till then, I'd been planning to spend a few days writing a narrative of events in the courtroom, concentrating on weaknesses in the prosecution case. I'd give my notes to Phil and he could write the first draft of the book while I was in Italy. He'd have plenty of media reports to pad it out with. Later, when Janet got back to me, we could get the family's angle on the case from her. I hadn't anticipated doing much more than that. But I was about to be persuaded otherwise.

'Did the defence grill this librarian?' Phil asked.

'The defence was a joke,' I said.

'You heard her in the witness box. Did she sound convincing?'

'The rest of the jury believed her. I didn't. She didn't seem at all sure. She might even have been guessing. But the defence didn't put any pressure on her, so the prosecution got away with it.'

'She'll have to be interviewed,' Phil said.

'You're pretty good at that sort of thing, aren't you?' I replied.

He shook his head. 'I've got script conferences in London, then I'm flying to Hollywood again. After that, it's New York for a convention on video games. I might be able to pop home now and again, but you'll have to do the spade work.'

That wasn't how I'd envisaged it.

'I'll give you sixty per cent of the advance and the royalties,' Phil said.

'You've already offered that.'

'Have I? Sixty-five, then. Final offer. What do you say, Tony?'

I thought about it. There could be spin-offs. Maybe there'd be a movie or a TV documentary. That meant good money. And with Clarissa and her lawyers on my back—

'OK,' I said. 'I'll do it.'

Phil grinned. 'Good lad. I look forward to working with you. Provided my agent gives me the thumbs-up. I'll draft something for her and email it off this afternoon. But don't be upset if she says no.'

4

Johnson Terrace is hidden away in a maze of tiny backstreets a few hundred yards from the waterfront at Riverwell. The Thames flows unconcernedly past before broadening into a choppy expanse that carries one of the heaviest densities of shipping in the world. The deep-water port at Tilbury, a few miles downstream from Riverwell, handles a wide range of bulk cargo and containers. Upstream, the Dartford Crossing spans the river like a row of pencils balanced end-to-end on rugby goalposts. When the wind is in the west, the low moan of its traffic can be heard in Johnson Terrace at all hours of the day and night.

Phil's agent didn't object to the book project, so I'd come to Riverwell to scope it out. I left my Volvo in the multi-storey car park in the high street and made my way to Johnson Terrace on foot. In less than ten minutes I was standing outside number 14. The property was an end-terrace that needed several licks of paint. The jury hadn't been taken to see it, but it was familiar to me from the photos we'd been shown. The tiny dwelling had been converted into flats, the ground floor becoming Flat 1 and the upstairs Flat 2. They were called flats, but they were like bedsitters – not much more than a room with a sink in the corner. No en suites, just a shared WC and bathroom in a single-storey extension to the rear. The extension housed the shared kitchen too.

Conrad and Doug had occupied the ground floor flat. The front garden was so tiny that I could have leaned over the low wall and touched the bay window. I couldn't see inside because it was boarded over with plywood, a leftover from the crime scene investigation. But I didn't need to. The photos of what the police found when they forced the door open were stamped on my memory: clothes scattered on the floor, unmade beds, Doug's easel with a half-finished painting on it, dirty crockery and cutlery littering every surface. And a dark stain on the carpet near the door.

That's where Doug had been lying, face down, clutching his chest, shot through the heart. After they saw that photo, several members of the jury refused to look at any more. They were probably wise. As the rest of us leafed through our folders, we encountered all sorts of horrors, not least the expression on Doug's face, photographed when the crime scene investigators turned his body over. He had been killed shortly after he got out of bed, it seemed, because he was still wearing his blue-

and-white joggers. There was a fluffy slipper on his left foot, but his right foot was bare. The missing slipper lay several yards away.

The prosecution made a lot of that nightwear. If Doug had been entertaining a visitor, Jolliffe insisted, he would have been fully dressed, probably in his usual garb of T-shirt and jeans. The fact that he'd been killed in his joggers suggested a domestic crime, and that put one person and one person only in the frame. There were no signs of a struggle. And the gun had been fired at point-blank range, suggesting that the killer was able to get close to Doug without arousing suspicion. Who do you allow that close when you're still wearing your pyjamas?

The awfulness of Doug's last moments filled my thoughts as I stood outside number 14. Maybe I stood there too long, because after a while I sensed that I was being watched. Looking round, I saw a woman staring at me from an upstairs window on the other side of the street. She could have thought I was a reporter. The area must have been teeming with them when the trial was in full swing.

I walked a few yards further down Johnson Terrace, then round the corner. This took me along the side of number 14. Out of sight from the prying neighbour, I stopped to inspect the back yard. It wasn't difficult because the boundary wall, a crumbling brick construction in need of repointing, was only about three feet high. There was no lawn for it to enclose, just bare earth trodden flat by many years of tenants' feet. Facing me on the far side of the yard was the single-storey extension that contained the shared WC, bathroom and kitchen. The kitchen door – through which the killer ran in panic when he fled the scene, according to Jolliffe – looked out on the yard. So did the rear window of Doug and Conrad's flat, now boarded up like the window at the front. Below it, a small patch of earth had been turned over. That must have been the flower bed where the killer had stopped to bury the murder weapon before disappearing down the road. It might have been full of flowers once. Now it was an ugly, churned-up mess.

'Can I help you?'

A woman's voice startled me out of my musing. I turned round and recognised her immediately. It was Mrs Drury, Doug and Conrad's landlady, a short woman with straight black hair and distrustful eyes. She'd been called as a character witness for Conrad at the trial. No doubt well-intentioned, she hadn't been much help. In her testimony, Mrs Drury said that Conrad kept himself to himself, paid the rent on time and seemed to be a nice young man. That was the best she could come up with. When she was cross-examined, Ursula Jolliffe didn't have much difficulty in establishing that Mrs Drury hardly knew him.

'Who are you? What do you want?' Mrs Drury was getting out her mobile phone as if to call 999. But it was reassuring that she hadn't recognised me from her brief appearance at the trial. That was the advantage of tucking myself away on the back row of the jury box.

'Quirke,' I said. 'My name is Tony Quirke.'
'And?'

'I'm looking for somewhere to rent.' Although the hotel was a dump, the weekly rate wasn't exactly reasonable. I needed to find another place soon. It might be sensible, I reckoned, to move close to the crime scene. It would give me a legitimate reason for being in the area if anyone asked me what I was up to.

Mrs Drury's suspicion vanished. 'You should have come to the office,' she said. The mobile phone went back in her pocket. 'These flats are very comfortable, very nice inside.' A generous sweep of her hand took in the slummy back yard and the ugly extension. Pulling out a business card, she handed it to me with a bashful smile.

Drury Properties
Arthur and Maeve Drury
For Sale and Let
Houses – Studio Flats – Holiday Homes – Caravans

'This one's vacant,' she said, indicating the murder flat.

I looked at the boarded-up window and said, 'Do you get a lot of vandals around here?'

'Oh no, nothing like that,' Mrs Drury said. 'The flat's being redecorated. It's getting new carpets throughout. It should be available in a week or so, ten days at the outside. There's a kitchen and a bathroom with all the facilities. When did you want to move in?'

I wasn't surprised they were laying new carpets. 'As soon as possible,' I said. 'I'm in temporary accommodation at the moment. Can I have a look inside?'

My request wasn't welcome. 'That might be difficult – we're still waiting for the decorators.' Mrs Drury pulled out a bunch of keys. 'But there's another vacancy next door, number 12. The top flat. They're exactly the same. Would you like to see it?'

Next door to the murder house would suit me fine. I followed Mrs Drury back round the corner, past number 14 and into the front garden of number 12. She unlocked the front door and I stepped into the hall. There was a damp smell and the paintwork was shabby, but at least the wallpaper and carpeting looked new.

'Go along up,' she said.

Feeling that I was stepping several decades back in time, I climbed the creaking stairs to the top flat. Mrs Drury followed and opened it for me. It was a smallish room with windows front and rear. I made a show of inspecting the heavy oak table, straight-backed chair, wardrobe and single bed, then made my way to the front window. Johnson Terrace lay beneath me. An elderly man was hobbling past on one of those aluminium walking sticks old folk get from the NHS. Further down the street, two kids were play-fighting with pieces of wood. A young woman came into view pushing a buggy. This seemed to be the main route to the high street from the houses down by the river. Surely plenty of people would have been out and about on a Saturday morning, the day of the murder? Even at ten past eight? Yet the prosecution had only produced one witness to the time of the shot. Why?

With Mrs Drury watching my every move, I went to the window at the rear and looked down on the back yard. It was separated from number 14's by a sturdy fence, but it was just as neglected. The accommodation was even worse than the hotel, but I said, 'Oh yes, this will do nicely.' Mrs Drury smiled at the compliment. After taking me downstairs to inspect the kitchen, bathroom and WC, none of which was any more impressive than what I'd seen upstairs, she said, 'Better come to the office.'

I followed her across the street and down an alley until we came to a corner shop. It had a sign over the door that said *Drury Properties*. The window was filled by a pinboard covered with rows of coloured cards. Mrs Drury unlocked the door, invited me in and plonked herself behind a computer. We did the legal stuff, then I paid my deposit, handed over the first month's rent and walked out with the keys to number 12.

Returning along the alley to Johnson Terrace, I turned right towards the high street. My intention was to explore the area thoroughly. An elderly lady was trudging towards me with a full shopping bag, so I offered to carry it home for her. She allowed me the privilege and I humped it a quarter of a mile. It wasn't the kindness of my heart. Phil had said he wanted local colour for the book, so I needed to meet as many people as possible. I wanted the residents to think of me as 'that nice young man from number 12'. There were bound to be plenty of Johnson Terrace folk who'd known Doug and Conrad. I wanted to hear what they had to say.

After leaving the old lady at her doorstep, I walked back along Johnson Terrace towards the high street.

Instead of continuing in that direction, as Conrad would have done on the morning of the murder, I stopped halfway and looked all around me. A narrow road off to the left led to the river. The houses were the same tiny terraces as the one I'd rented a room in, but what had caught my eye was a pub.

The Swan, the sign said in Old English capitals. The picture was a Thames sailing barge heeling over in the wind. They do look rather swan-like in full sail, although I've never seen a swan with brown wings.

Inside, the pub wasn't roomy but it was warm and welcoming. The white plaster on the walls had taken on a yellow tinge, the artificial beams were coated with dust and the lattice windows were dirty enough to look original. The décor couldn't have suited the locality better if it had been planned that way.

The landlord, who would have been six-foot-six if he stood up straight, was leaning over the bar reading a newspaper.

'A pint of best bitter in a straight glass, please,' I said.

He folded the newspaper, shoved it under the bar, pulled my pint and placed it on a fresh beer mat in front of me. The only other customer was a woman in her forties or fifties perched on a stool beside me. She was gazing into her glass and didn't seem to have noticed my presence. Not wanting to disturb her, I carried my drink to a battered Formica-covered table, sat down, took a sip and began to plan how I was going to take things forward.

With its jerry-built houses, concreted-over front gardens and the reputation Phil had given it, Riverwell was the ideal setting for the kind of book I was hoping we would write. I was relying on Phil's flair with words to bring it to life, and felt confident he would do a good job. He was at the top of his game. My own job was to get the facts together. There was no better time to start than now, so in the back of my diary, the only notebook I had on me, I wrote:

Conrad's landlady, Mrs Drury: did her best for him at the trial. Not enough to offset the damaging picture Jolliffe painted of him, though. Windows still boarded up

– and the other details I've mentioned, including the nosey parker across the street. There wasn't going to be any shortage of local colour.

Finishing my pint, I went to the bar for another. This time the landlord was more talkative.

'Passing through?' he asked as he eased the hand pump back. He was in his fifties or sixties with grey hair, a pencil moustache and a deeply lined face.

'I'm moving in,' I said, 'round the corner. Johnson Terrace, number 12.' I don't normally give my address to strangers, but like I said, I wanted to get known.

The middle-aged woman looked up from her glass. She was heavily made up, with an expensive honey-coloured hairdo. I gave her a smile but it wasn't returned. She studied me through large, stylish glasses as if she didn't approve of what she saw. 'Oh my God, you haven't moved into Drury Towers, have you?' she said in a husky voice that spoke of a lifetime of chain-smoking.

I must have appeared taken aback. 'She doesn't mean anything by it,' the landlord said quickly. 'She was only pulling your leg. Give over, Mary, let the gentleman enjoy his drink.'

'Drury Towers?' I asked.

'She means Johnson Terrace,' the landlord said. 'Numbers 12 and 14.'

The woman continued to stare at me.

'Tony Quirke's the name,' I said.

'Len Mackle,' the landlord replied. 'Pleased to meet you. And may I present Mrs Mary McGurk?'

This time I got a smile.

'Hello, Mrs McGurk,' I said. 'Drury Towers, is that what it's called? That's news to me. There was a vacancy in number 14, but I didn't fancy it.'

'I'm not surprised,' Mrs McGurk said, and returned her gaze to the bottom of her glass.

'You know what happened, I suppose?' said Len.

'Oh yes. It was on the news.'

'Blood everywhere, was what I heard.'

'But some people doubt the verdict,' I said.

'Do they?' Len seemed surprised, then glanced over my shoulder at the door. A man in a bomber jacket had come in. He had the tanned skin of someone who works long hours out of doors.

'Morning, Ian,' said Len, starting to run draught Guinness into a pint glass.

I decided to jump straight in. 'Do you think Connor actually did the murder?' I asked Len.

'What do you think, Ian?' he said. 'We're talking about the Drury Towers murder.'

'Connor did it all right,' said Ian.

Len kept his eyes on the Guinness. 'There's not many round here think different,' he said.

Ian smoothed back his hair as he watched the Guinness creep up the side of the glass. 'They were at it day and night,' he said, 'those two.'

'At what?' I said.

'At each other's throats like shithouse rats.'

'Is that so?' I said. 'I never heard.'

'You hear all sorts,' said Len.

'Good riddance,' said Ian. 'Both of them.'

'Connor was on the checkouts at Asda,' Mrs McGurk broke in. 'Creepy little bugger. I always avoided him, even if it meant joining a longer queue. When the shooting come on the news, I thought, Hello, he's gone and done it at last. Just as well I wasn't around when he snapped.'

Nobody spoke after that. Len opened his newspaper and continued reading. Ian supped his Guinness. Mrs McGurk took a tissue out of her handbag and dabbed her lips with it.

'Oh well,' I said, 'it takes all sorts.'

'I don't know about that,' said Mrs McGurk, 'but Margery had a narrow escape. She was at her sister's when it happened.'

'Margery?' I said.

'Miss Prim,' said Len without looking up from his paper. 'Their upstairs neighbour.'

I nearly spilled my pint. *He didn't do it – ask Miss Prim.* This was incredible. I could never have guessed how much I'd learn in such a short space of time. All I had to do was walk into the local. Miss Prim was my next-door neighbour? The mysterious woman who knew that Conrad didn't do it, but hadn't appeared at the trial? She went straight to the top of my interview list. I was so pleased I bought everyone a drink.

'Cheers, mate,' said Ian, looking me in the face for the first time. Mrs McGurk even called me 'darling' as Len handed over her dry Martini. She always drank it with ice and a slice of lemon, she told me, as if she was letting me into a secret. And after that I really did belong.

5

It was a cold and windy day when I moved out of my hotel and into number 12, but at least the rain was holding off. At first, the thought of sunlight dappling the waters of the Venetian canals made me regret sacrificing my holiday. But I was soon over it and raring to go. It was an easy move – Clarissa's thoughtfulness in kicking me out of the bungalow with just one Volvo-full of belongings meant it only required a single trip.

Even so, I wasn't going to have much room. Although my new home had been created by knocking the front and back bedrooms into one, they'd both been small to begin with. The flat was an even tighter squeeze than the hotel. On the other hand, it was light and airy, and I had a grand view of the river from the rear window – if I stood on a chair. I could also see into the back yard of the murder house next door. There was washing on the line, so it looked as if Miss Prim was home.

A familiar melody came faintly through the dividing wall. I knew the signature tune of *The Archers* only too well, because Clarissa never missed an episode. It seemed that Miss Prim had switched on her radio. I didn't want to spoil her enjoyment, so I waited until the programme ended before I went next door and rang her bell.

After a long wait, footsteps came shuffling along the hall. The front door opened and I got my first sight of Miss Prim. She was an old lady, thin and rather frail, with glasses, silver hair and watery eyes.

'Yes?' she said cautiously.

A little lie doesn't do much harm in these situations. 'I don't want to bother you,' I said, 'but I'm looking for accommodation. Mrs Drury said there was a vacancy here.' I pointed to the boarded front window of Doug and Conrad's flat.

Miss Prim looked bewildered.

'Do you mind if I have a quick peek?' I said.

She didn't reply, just carried on looking bewildered.

I could see along the passage and into the kitchen. Remembering the photos we were shown at the trial, I recognised the route the killer supposedly took after he shot Doug – out of Flat 1, along the passage, down the single step to the kitchen and into the yard. If Miss Prim had been home, she might have got a good look at him. She would certainly have known the time of the shot. But of course, she'd been at her sister's.

'I only want to cast my eyes over it,' I said.

'Didn't Ma give you the keys?'

As I found out later, the Drury Towers tenants all referred to Mrs Drury as Ma.

'She gave me the keys to the top flat next door,' I said and held them up. The Drury Properties tag proved that I was genuine. 'But if the ground floor is vacant here, I'd like to look at that one too.'

Miss Prim still didn't know how to take me.

'I'm sorry,' I said, turning to leave. 'I shouldn't have disturbed you. I'll go back to the agency and ask Mrs Drury to show me round later.'

That was all it took. You only need to convince them you're not a burglar or a salesman and you're in.

'Well,' Miss Prim said, rubbing her chin, 'I suppose so.'

Once inside, my eyes went straight to the door to Flat 1. It was scarred by jemmy marks where the police had forced their entry. A patch of carpet had been cut away in front of it, revealing bare boards dotted with ancient drops of paint. A faint smell of disinfectant hung in the air like a ghost.

'I suppose Ma told you what happened,' Miss Prim said.

'Oh yes. Dreadful, wasn't it?'

'You won't get into their flat,' she said. 'I don't know why Ma told you it's available, because it won't be ready for weeks. The police wouldn't let anyone touch it while the trial was on.'

'I must have misunderstood her,' I said. 'My mistake.'

'I can show you the kitchen and bathroom, if you like.'

'Could you? That would be very kind.'

I followed Miss Prim along the narrow passageway into the kitchen.

'We have to keep it tidy,' she said. 'The boys never did. That was the only thing I had against them.'

The kitchen was best described as basic. I'm not sure how Ma Drury would have justified her claim that it had all the facilities. Miss Prim opened the half-glazed door that led to the bathroom and WC, then stood aside to let me through. But I had my eyes on the door that led to the yard.

'Would you like to see outside?' she said, noticing my interest.

'If it's not too much bother.'

I stepped into the yard and tried to imagine Conrad emerging from the house after killing Doug, stopping to bury the murder weapon in the flower bed, then making off for the station as fast as he could. It didn't stack up. If he was fleeing in panic, as Jolliffe had claimed, would he have wasted time trying to hide the weapon? And in such an obvious place, under the rear window of his own flat?

'It needs a few flowers,' I said when I went inside again. 'Wisteria would look nice against that wall.'

'Or gypsophila,' Miss Prim said. 'Do you like gypsophila? Baby's breath, it's called.'

'Yes, I know. It's pretty, isn't it?'

'Will you have a cup of tea?' Miss Prim asked. She was warming to me already.

'Thank you. I don't mind if I do.'

She filled an electric kettle, opened a wall cabinet and got out a tea caddy. 'This one is mine,' she said, pointing to the tidy arrangement of packets, tins and jars in the cabinet. 'You'd keep your things there.' She indicated the cabinet next to it. I tried to imagine what Doug and Conrad had filled it with.

'Don't you feel uneasy,' I said, 'living here after what happened?'

Miss Prim gave me a funny look.

'Knowing that you shared a kitchen—'

She shook her head. 'They were nice boys. Despite what people say.' She made the tea and we sat down at a little folding table.

'I heard they didn't get on,' I said as Miss Prim offered me a biscuit. I was remembering what Ian had said. And the testimony of Doug's mother, the woman who made the impassioned statement on the courthouse steps after Conrad was convicted. At the trial, she'd told us how jealous Conrad had been of her poor Douglas. She'd met him several times, she said, and could see it in his eyes. She even told us about the disturbing dreams she'd been having, dreams that one day Conrad would do serious harm to her son. I wasn't persuaded that dreams counted as evidence, but they impressed my fellow jurors. There's nothing like a grieving mother to melt the coldest heart.

'You don't want to believe the papers,' Miss Prim said. 'Douglas and Conrad got on very well.'

That came as a surprise. 'Surely there was bound to be rivalry,' I said, 'with both of them artists, one successful and one not?'

'I know what you're trying to say,' Miss Prim said, 'but you're wrong. They were very close. Always doing things for each other. Douglas took on extra work at Fearings when the supermarket reduced Conrad's hours. They couldn't have managed otherwise.'

'Fearings?' I said.

'Fearings of Purfleet. They're builders' merchants. My father knew the original Mr Fearing in the 1950s. He set up the business by himself, but after the war…'

I listened attentively. I didn't want to give the impression that I wasn't interested in Mr Fearing and his family business. But when Miss Prim paused to take a sip of tea, I said, 'I didn't know that Doug worked in a builders' merchants. I thought he was an artist. You mean he was humping bricks and sacks of cement as well?'

Miss Prim shook her head. 'He didn't have the physique for it, did he?' she said. 'No, Douglas was a watchman. He worked most weekends and occasional nights. They needed the money, you see. Conrad didn't earn much. But then Douglas got to know someone in London. The owner of an art gallery, he said. A very kind gentleman. He put Douglas's paintings up for sale and all of a sudden Douglas was in the money. He was talking of buying a sports car, would you believe. Just imagine – Douglas in a sports car!'

It was very interesting, but I wanted to get back to the relationship between the flatmates. 'Conrad must have felt jealous when Doug got all that recognition,' I said.

Miss Prim furrowed her brow. 'No, no, no. Conrad was only too happy when Douglas was taken on by the gallery. No jealousy at all. I knew Conrad as if he was my own son. He came running up the stairs to tell me the good news. He was as pleased as punch.'

I wasn't sure how far to believe her. Would Miss Prim have seen enough of her downstairs neighbours to know how well they got on? Even though she shared the 'facilities' with them? She might not have been able to hear them arguing – judging by how high she turned up her radio, she was probably slightly deaf. And she didn't seem the sort of person to give anyone a bad name.

'Something serious must have happened,' I said, 'to make Conrad put a gun to Doug's chest.'

Miss Prim looked offended. 'Conrad? Shoot Douglas? Why on earth would he want to do such a thing?'

'That's the conclusion the court came to,' I said. 'They decided he was a cold-blooded murderer.'

'You shouldn't say things like that. He never was … what you said. Not poor Conrad.' Miss Prim stared down into empty hands, overcome with emotion. 'Conrad thought the world of Douglas.' She raised her eyes to look at me. Glazed with tears, they made her words all the more convincing.

'Didn't you mention it to the police?' I said. 'How well they got on together?'

A dark cloud seemed to drift across Miss Prim's face. 'Oh yes. The police practically moved in. They questioned me over and over again.'

'It must have been stressful,' I said, 'giving evidence

at the trial.' I was aware that she hadn't, but I didn't want her to know that.

'I wasn't asked,' she said.

'You weren't *asked?*

She looked mystified, as if she couldn't understand why I was so startled by her reply. 'I suppose it was because I wasn't at home when it happened,' she said.

I'd been assuming she'd been too nervous to give evidence, or that she'd been ill, or that she'd had some other reason for staying away. But if the prosecution had decided not to call her as a witness, they should have disclosed her evidence to the defence. Then the defence could have put her up against Mrs Hamilton.

We continued to talk about everyday, inconsequential things – putting the bins out, local shops, trouble with mice. But all the time my mind was turning over the implications of what Miss Prim had said. I recognised a whole bundle of them. *There is no doubt in my mind that your motive was jealousy of your flatmate's success,* the judge had thundered at Conrad. *I have heard convincing evidence of this.* Convincing evidence? Why hadn't Miss Prim appeared before the court to give the opposing view? Had the police been cherry-picking evidence that supported the prosecution, ignoring anything which implied that Conrad was innocent? I had no way of knowing. It was possible that they'd passed Miss Prim's evidence to the defence, and for reasons of their own the defence had decided not to use her. But it was a major oversight, whoever was at fault, because all the jury heard about the Conrad-Doug relationship came from Mrs Hamilton.

Back in number 12, I wrote up my notes for Phil. We now knew that Doug had had a job. Jolliffe had given us the impression he spent all his time at the easel, but that wasn't the way things had been. I wasn't sure how much it told us, but at least the Fearings job would enable Phil to write about Doug in a more rounded way. Phil liked rounded characters.

Jolliffe might have kept the Fearings job quiet, but she made a song and dance about Doug's contract with the Willoughby Gallery. I got out my phone and visited its website in search of his work. Three of his paintings were up for sale. I'd been expecting something abstract or off the wall, the sort of thing I supposed all modern artists did. Not Doug Hamilton. *Carnations* was half a dozen pretty blooms in a vase, painted with photographic realism. The others were *Spring Bouquet* and *Kingfisher* – you can guess what they were like. In a way, Doug's artwork defined him. They were gentle, homely pictures, the sort that little old ladies treasure, and they made his murder seem all the more senseless. The prices ranged from £250 to £500. He must have sold a good number of them to be thinking of buying a sports car.

Finishing off my notes, I decided I'd done enough for one day. It was time for a pie and a pint. If the Swan was going to be my local, I'd better start using it. Tomorrow I'd check out Conrad's alibi. My next port of call would be Colchester.

6

I'd already seen Wes Lubbock in the witness box. 'Unsympathetic' would be a generous assessment of his attitude to Conrad, the man who was supposed to be his friend. Conrad had always denied he was running away when he went to visit him on the morning of the murder. Wes had been expecting him, he said. But at the trial Wes swore on oath that he hadn't. This allowed Jolliffe to paint Conrad as a liar, which she did with withering scorn, casting doubt on everything he said. The effect on the jury was devastating. 'That's it, he's guilty as fuck,' one of my fellow jurors muttered under his breath. As far as he was concerned, the matter was settled and no further discussion could make him change his mind. Wes had done Conrad a lot of damage. So I was expecting the meeting to be a difficult one.

I knew which street he lived on in Colchester – it

was mentioned at the trial – but not the house number. According to my maps app, Pearl Street ran parallel to the river that bisects this ancient Roman city, once the nation's capital. I walked there from the station, smelling the river before I rounded a corner and found myself on a quayside. No doubt a picturesque little community in the days of sail, the area was now a huddle of industrial estates and social housing.

Pearl Street was a cul-de-sac, wedged between a scrapyard and a block of retirement homes. I started knocking on doors from number 1 onwards. No one seemed to be at home. The first three residents who answered said they had never heard of Wes Lubbock. It wasn't until number 11 that an old woman struggled to the door on a walking frame and told me Yes, she knew Mr Lubbock. He lived at number 17, she said.

I spotted Wes through the front window of his house, bent over a dark object in what I soon discovered to be his living room. He answered the door with a woodworking tool in his hand – a spokeshave, I think it's called – and a sour expression on his face. He was tall and thin, with long brown hair and an untrimmed beard.

'I'm a friend of the Connor family,' I said. 'My name is Tony Quirke. I was wondering if I could have a brief word.'

'What about?'

'About what happened,' I said. The sour look didn't change, so I added, 'Maybe you haven't heard. After he was sentenced, Conrad took his own life. It was a terrible shock for the family. His sister has asked me—'

'Do you mean Janet?'

'That's right,' I said. 'Do you know her?'

'I knew her,' Wes said, 'a long time ago.'

I got the impression he didn't want anything to do with the Connor family or their misfortunes. It was the attitude he'd shown in the witness box. 'Can I come in?' I said.

Wes hesitated, then stood aside for me. The front door opened directly on the living room. It was only then that I recognised the dark object Wes had been bending over. It was a boat, a small dinghy, bottom-up on trestles. The furniture had been pushed back to the walls to make room for it. There was a smell of newly sawn wood and the carpet was strewn with shavings.

'Nice,' I said, looking at the boat. It was beautifully finished. I would have judged it ready for its first coat of varnish. Wes ran his hand along the keel, pausing here and there to explore the surface with the tips of his fingers.

'Keen on sailing, are you?' I said.

'This is for a customer,' he said gruffly. Bending over the keel, he resumed work with the spokeshave as if I wasn't there. 'What can I do for you?' he asked after a while, without looking at me or interrupting the steady rhythm of his strokes.

'Can we talk about Conrad Connor for a moment?' I said.

Wes shrugged. He put down the spokeshave, slapped the dust off his overalls and opened a sliding glass door on the far side of the room. I followed him through to the kitchen. It was spacious, what estate agents call a farmhouse kitchen. One wall was covered with bookshelves from top to bottom, and there was a table with chairs round it. I sat on one of the chairs while Wes pulled the sliding door shut. There was a book on the table. I picked it up and looked at the cover. It was about a round-the-world yachting race.

'I've never done any sailing myself,' I said, putting it down again.

Wes grunted. He was a surly character. Instead of joining me at the table, he went to the sink, ran himself a glass of tap water and took a sip. 'The dust gets in your throat,' he explained with his back to me.

'Why don't you wear a mask?' I said.

He took another sip without replying, then carried his half-empty glass to the table. Seating himself opposite me, he said, 'What did you want to know about Conrad?'

I got straight to the point. 'As I told you, the reason I'm here is Janet. What has made Conrad's death so much worse for her is the belief that he was innocent. She's asked me to help clear his name. I was hoping you could tell me about the day he came to see you.'

Wes stood up so fast that he knocked over his glass, sending a stream of water shooting across the table. I moved the sailing book out of the way just in time.

'There's nothing I can do about clearing Conrad's name,' he said, mopping the table with the sleeve of his jumper.

I grabbed some kitchen roll from the draining board and finished the job for him. 'That's OK,' I said. 'I only wanted to talk about it.'

'I can't see why you came to me,' he said, sitting down again. 'I hardly knew Conrad Connor. He was in the sailing club – they both were – but that was years ago. I had nothing to do with him after that.'

'I hear what you're saying,' I said, 'but Janet Connor is shattered. If you could see the state she's in, you'd be horrified. Can you imagine what it's like when your brother hangs himself? I was hoping you could fill in a few things about the day he visited you. Janet would be more than grateful.'

Wes took his time considering my request. He must have decided it was reasonable. 'That's right,' he said, 'Conrad did turn up on my doorstep. It was a surprise. But there's nothing more I can tell you.'

'He stayed the night?'

Wes flushed. 'I thought he'd been kicked out of his accommodation and didn't have anywhere to go. I couldn't slam the door in his face, could I? Yes, he stayed the night. But there was no way he could move in.'

'Why did he come to see you?' I asked.

'I don't know. He didn't say much. He seemed to think we were great pals, but like I said, I hadn't seen him for years. I told him straight that there wasn't enough room for him. He left the next morning.' Wes was breathing heavily. I'd been right. This was going to be difficult.

'Can you enlighten me about one thing,' I said, 'so I can tell Janet I've done my best? At the trial, Conrad said that you were expecting him. But you said you weren't. Are you sure about that?'

'Yes,' said Wes. 'Absolutely.'

'Your testimony was one of the things that convicted him,' I said. 'Because if he lied about that, how could anyone believe anything else he said?'

'Careful,' Wes snapped. 'I told the police what happened, no more and no less. Have you ever had them lean on you? First thing I know, there's a couple of policemen at the door. "We want to talk to you about your friend Conrad Connor." He wasn't my friend, but no one seems capable of understanding that.'

'What did you tell them?'

'I told them what happened. Conrad turned up on my doorstep on the Saturday. No, I hadn't invited him. No, I didn't know he was coming. No, he wasn't my friend. I hadn't seen him for years.' Wes bit his thumb. 'I had no idea what he'd already said to them. If I'd known, I might—' He left the sentence unfinished, took his thumb out of his mouth and examined the nail. There was blood on it.

He was sticking to the story he had told at the trial, but I could see that something was troubling him.

'If he had your address,' I said, 'he must have known you.'

'Look,' said Wes, getting heated again, 'I haven't the slightest idea why he got in touch.'

'Is there any possibility that you did agree to meet beforehand?'

Wes looked away. Then he said, 'No.'

'But you said he *got in touch,*' I said. 'What did you mean by that? Got in touch before his visit?'

Wes got up, went to the sink and stood with his back

to me again. There wasn't much to see out of the window – a raised border, an ugly breezeblock wall. When he spoke, all the bluster had gone.

'He sent me a birthday card, yes. But I had no idea he was going to come knocking on my door.'

'Sent you a birthday card?' It was difficult to keep the astonishment out of my voice. 'When?'

'A couple of weeks before he came. What's so odd about sending a card? That's what people do when it's your birthday, isn't it? I don't know why. He hadn't sent me one for years. Not even a Christmas card. Yeah, he sent me a card. But his visit was a total surprise. I definitely hadn't invited him. How many times have I got to tell you that?'

I was in danger of pushing him too far. 'Thanks,' I said and stood up. 'I won't waste any more of your time.'

Looking relieved, Wes opened the sliding door to let me out of the kitchen. But I had no intention of leaving. I wanted to see the birthday card. At the trial, we were given the impression that Conrad hadn't contacted Wes before his visit. But if he'd sent Wes a card, that was contact. I stopped halfway to the front door.

'I don't suppose you kept it?' I said. 'The card, I mean?'

'What's that to you?'

'I'd like Janet to have it,' I said. 'She's keeping things to remember Conrad by. There isn't much.'

'You said you were going.'

I took a few more steps towards the front door. But I wasn't going to give up yet. 'If you could see the state Janet's got herself into—'

'Now that Conrad's dead,' Wes said, 'there's nothing

that can be done.' He walked to the stern of the boat and ran his hands over the flat part where the outboard motor goes. This time he didn't touch the spokeshave. I waited while his conscience got to work on him.

'I told the truth,' he said. 'But the police don't give you a chance. They were in here firing questions at me, writing down everything I said. Then they got me to sign it. They never told me what it was about. At first, I thought they were after me, not Conrad. But I gave them an honest answer: "Were you expecting him? No, I wasn't." That's all I can tell you. Sorry.' He picked up the spokeshave and went to work. But his movements were slow, as if there was something he still hadn't told me. I couldn't guess why the police might have been after him, but that didn't concern me. I wanted to find out what he was holding back.

'The card,' I said.

The spokeshaving stopped. 'If I give it to you, will you leave me out of whatever you're up to?'

'It's Janet I'm thinking of,' I said.

'That's not an answer. If I give you the card, will that be the end of it?'

I rested my hands on the sharp end of the boat. 'This is about helping Janet get through the nightmare of losing her brother,' I said. 'So yes, let me have the card and that's the last you'll hear from me.'

Wes was breathing heavily again. 'How do I know you'll keep your word?'

'I have no reason to lie to you. What else can I say?'

He pointed the spokeshave at me. 'If you do drag me into this, you'll regret it.'

'That's fair enough by me,' I said.

He looked at me as if he was still undecided, then balanced the spokeshave on the keel of the boat. 'Through here,' he said and went back into the kitchen. I followed.

He went straight to the bookshelves and ran his eyes along them. They were stuffed with all sorts of odds and ends as well as books – box files, printer cartridges, a mug full of ballpoint pens. He took down a manila file and started to sort through it. There were press cuttings, old envelopes, receipts, a booklet about the World Sailing Competition – and finally some greetings cards. He looked through them until he came to what he was after. Fizzing champagne flutes danced merrily round *Happy Birthday* in fancy lettering. I stretched out my hand for it. He kept it out of reach.

'This was his,' he said.

'Can I see inside?'

He opened the card and showed it to me. It was from Conrad, no doubt about that. He'd signed it in a large, almost childlike script below the printed *Have a Good One* message. And below his signature he'd added a few words of his own.

Seems ages since Maldon!!! OK if I drop by some time?

It was too late, far too late.

'Do you realise what this means?' I said. 'Conrad was telling the truth. He didn't run for the train in panic after shooting Doug. He'd been thinking of paying you a visit. He'd written to you asking if he could drop by.'

Wes stared at the card as if he was reading it for the first time. The disbelief on his face gave way to fury. I looked round for an escape route. But all he said was, 'Can't you get it into your head? I wasn't expecting him.'

'He thought you were,' I said, risking it.

Wes glared at me. 'I never wrote to him and said, "Thanks for the card, when are you coming?" I couldn't stand the prat.'

'Why didn't you tell the police about it?' I said.

There was no reply. As I watched Wes get angrier and angrier, I could only guess what must have happened. When he received the card, Conrad's enquiry about the possibility of dropping by hadn't registered. He couldn't stand the prat. So it was a surprise when Conrad arrived on his doorstep two weeks later. And when the police interviewed him, he told them he hadn't been expecting him, which was true. It was a misunderstanding, one which the tongue-tied Conrad was unable to explain in the witness box. And if Wes had remembered the card after the trial, he hadn't seen fit to do anything about it. There wouldn't have been any point. By then, Conrad was dead.

'Look mate,' Wes said through clenched teeth, 'when I made my statement, I had no idea that Conrad was using me as an alibi. No one told me anything. I wasn't allowed to attend the trial before I went into the witness box. And then all they asked was, "Were you expecting him?"'

'Can I have the card?' I said.

Wes was still holding it out of reach. He read Conrad's message again, then stepped across to the sink, tore the card into pieces and stuffed it down the plughole. Stretching out his arm, he pressed a switch on the wall. The metallic shriek of a waste disposal unit ended the possibility of further negotiations.

'The door's over there,' he said.

7

I'd come away from Colchester without the card, and I was sure that Wes would never testify to having received it. But a radically different story was beginning to emerge. What I'd found out didn't prove that Conrad was innocent, but the scales of justice were tilting in his favour. So I was in an upbeat mood when I got back to number 12 and found a workman in the hall. There was a bag of tools at his feet and a pair of stepladders leaning against the banisters.

'Problem?' I asked.

Well into his seventies, his hair stuck down with Brylcreem or something similar, the workman had the appearance of a dance band leader from the Benny Goodman era.

'Tenant in Flat 1 complaining about knocking pipes,' he said. Reaching into the bag of tools, he took out a wrench, bent down and disappeared into the cramped space under the stairs. 'When we moved the bathroom to the ground floor,' his voice echoed back, 'we had to reroute the cold water. That's the cause of it.' The wrench clanged against metal. 'Sorry to spoil your peace and quiet, but it won't take long.'

'It's no bother,' I said and started climbing the stairs to my flat. I'd reached the top when the clanging stopped and the workman called after me.

'You must be Mr Quirke.'

He was standing at the foot of the stairs holding out his hand, so I went down again. As we shook, I noticed that the top section of his index finger was missing. It didn't seem to have cramped his style with the wrench.

'Call me Tony,' I said.

'And I'm Arthur,' he replied. 'Mrs Drury's other half.'

He looked a cheerful, obliging sort of chap. You could do worse for a landlord, I thought.

'Everything all right?' he asked, pointing up the stairs.

'Very comfortable,' I said. 'It's beginning to feel like home already.' I didn't want to say what I thought of his squalid little flat. If it hadn't been next door to the murder site, I wouldn't have given it a second glance.

'Any problems, give me a ring. You can always get me at the office.'

'As a matter of fact,' I said, 'there is something I wanted to ask you.'

He gave me a grin. 'Nothing too big, nothing too small.'

'I spoke to Mrs Drury about moving next door,' I said, stretching it the way I had with Miss Prim. 'Number 14, the downstairs flat. I was wondering when it was likely to be available.'

'Well,' he said, looking pleased that I was taking an interest, 'it's bigger than the one you're in now. The bay window adds quite a lot. Surprising, isn't it?' He stretched out his arms. 'A few extra feet, but it adds a whole new dimension to a room.'

'It's not the bay window,' I said. 'I fancied being downstairs.'

'It'll be available soon,' he said. 'Same rent, but you'll have to wait a week or so, maybe longer. It's the decorators – they were supposed to be here yesterday.' He sounded apologetic, then frowned. 'You do know what happened, don't you?'

'I do,' I said. 'Tragic, wasn't it?'

'But you wouldn't mind living there? Wouldn't give you the collywobbles?'

'Not if the place had been put right,' I said. 'Once it's done up, I'd be happy to move in.'

He looked relieved. 'You're the first person to say that. The publicity hasn't done us any favours, I can tell you. Nasty piece of work, Connor. But he's gone now.'

'Did you know him well?' I asked. 'He was an artist, or so I heard.'

Arthur Drury laughed. 'As much of an artist as I am. No, it's good to see the back of him. There's no troublemakers in any of the flats now, you can rest assured of that.'

'It's nice to know,' I said. 'But to be perfectly frank, I've heard rumours that it wasn't Connor who did the murder.'

The friendly attitude disappeared.

'I read about the case in the papers,' I said. 'The evidence seemed pretty weak to me. They didn't even find his fingerprints on the gun.'

Drury was giving me a cold stare.

'Someone else must have done it,' I said.

As I was to learn later, Arthur Drury was an East Ender of the old school, a man who loved the sound of his own voice. On this occasion, I seemed to have silenced him.

'It's hard to believe,' I said, 'letting off a gun in a flat. The whole street must have heard.'

Landlords don't like talking about blood being spilled on their properties, least of all to potential tenants, but I wasn't going to let that stop me. Pointing to my downstairs neighbour's door, I said, 'I wonder if he heard it?' The nameplate said *George*. There wasn't a surname. I'd heard him coming and going, but I hadn't had a chance to meet him.

Drury's eyes followed the direction of my finger, rather reluctantly I thought. For a moment or two we stared at George's door in silence. Drury needed to get the decorators at work there too. The paint was chipped and there were scuff marks along the bottom.

'He heard it all right,' Drury said. 'He made me fix a new lock. He's the nervous type.'

'He heard it? Did he say what time?'

The expression on Drury's face was now positively hostile. I could have been asking what he and Mrs Drury got up to in the marital bedroom. He wasn't going to answer me, but I wasn't bothered. He'd already told me more than he realised.

'It's been nice meeting you, Mr Drury,' I said.

'I'll let you know when next door's ready,' he said, picking up the bag of tools. I held the front door open for him while he hoisted the stepladders on his shoulder. The friendly grin I gave him as he left wasn't returned.

I climbed the stairs to my flat wondering why Janet hadn't called me back. Several days had passed since I phoned her and I'd heard nothing. I supposed it was the shock of losing her brother. She'd experienced a devastating bereavement in the most terrible of circumstances. But I was desperate to speak to her so I phoned her again. As before, all I got was her voicemail, so I left her another message. 'Tony Quirke here,' I said. 'I know you probably want to be left alone at a time like this. But I'd like to talk to you, if it's at all possible, because there have been some important developments. Nothing can bring Conrad back, I know, but I think there's a chance of clearing his name. If that's what you want. And I'd like to help you, if you'll let me.' I told her that I'd moved to Riverwell, and what I'd been doing there. I didn't let on about the book I was planning to write with Phil. That might have put her off. I restricted myself to my meetings with Miss Prim and Wes Lubbock, and how their stories had contradicted the prosecution case. 'Nobody would agree that Conrad got a fair trial if they knew what those two told me,' I said. 'And there's more. Mrs Wilderman wasn't the only person who heard the shot that killed Doug. My downstairs neighbour heard it too, would you believe? This is the most important lead yet. I haven't had a chance to speak to him, but I will. If you're able, give me a bell as soon as you can.'

Mrs Wilderman's testimony had been a disaster for the defence.

'What sort of a noise did you hear when you were passing the flat that morning?' Jolliffe asked her.

'A bang,' Mrs Wilderman said.

'Loud?'

'Not very.'

'The sound of a handgun being fired?'

'I didn't think so at the time,' Mrs Wilderman said. 'You don't want anything like that in Johnson Terrace, do you? It was like a child kicking a football against a garage door. That's what I thought it was. But now I know it must have been a gun.'

'What makes you certain it was a gun?' Jolliffe asked.

'The police took me to an army shooting range. They made me stand outside a building. Then they went inside and fired the murder weapon. It sounded exactly the same.'

'Exactly the same?'

'That's right.'

'Thank you,' said Jolliffe. 'What time did you hear this noise?'

Mrs Wilderman didn't answer.

Jolliffe waited, and when her witness remained silent, tried a prompt. 'In your statement to the police, you said it was ten past eight,' she said. 'Is that right?'

Mrs Wilderman still didn't answer. To my way of thinking, her silence said a lot. She was far from sure. Awkward seconds passed, then the judge intervened. 'You have to answer the question,' she said. 'What time did you hear the noise?'

Mrs Wilderman looked at Jolliffe, then at the judge, then at Jolliffe again. 'Ten past eight, I suppose.'

'Ten past eight,' Jolliffe repeated, in case the jury hadn't heard. 'And someone firing a gun inside number 14 Johnson Terrace at ten past eight could get to the station before the eight forty train departed?'

'I suppose so. It's only a ten minute walk.'

The defence's cross examination of Mrs Wilderman was half-hearted. They didn't have anything to throw at her. But now I hoped there might be. At around six thirty, I heard the occupant of Flat 1 return. I gave him a few minutes to sort himself out, then went downstairs and knocked on his door.

'Who is it?'

Arthur Drury had been right. George sounded the nervous type.

'I'm the new tenant who's moved in upstairs,' I said.

I had to wait while he drew back a heavy bolt and turned a key in the lock. When at last the door opened, I was met by a plump African about five-foot-six in height. He was wearing a yellow T-shirt and a New York Yankees baseball cap, also yellow. Bang on trend, my neighbour, quite a surprise.

'I thought I'd better say hello,' I said, 'now that we're sharing a kitchen and a bathroom. The name's Tony Quirke.'

'My name is George,' he said. I think he was pleased that I'd taken the trouble.

He'd put a lot of work into making his flat comfortable. The Drurys' second-hand furniture had been replaced by smart modern stuff, including two faux-leather easy chairs. There was a colourful carpet on the floor, and arty African posters on the walls. But he hadn't got rid of the smell of damp. I was beginning to recognise that as the Drury Towers trademark.

'This might not be the right moment,' I said, noticing a large cardboard box on one of the chairs – a brand-new sound system, judging by the label. George must have been about to unpack it. 'I can call back later, if you like.'

'No,' he said, 'sit down.' He lifted the box off the chair and deposited it on his bed.

While he made coffee in the sparkling new kitchenette he must have installed himself, I decided it wouldn't be wise to quiz him about the gunshot immediately. I needed to win his confidence first. So when we were seated with mugs of coffee in our hands, I told him about my job as an account executive at Williams Wells. We were one of the biggest collection agencies in the City, I explained, if not the biggest. And of course, I had to tell him what we collected. 'Has it turned you against me?' I said. That's the little quip I make when people discover what I do for a living.

George laughed. 'We have debt collectors at home,' he said. 'They're needed.' He told me that he hailed from Port Harcourt in Nigeria. His real name was Adedayo Ojukwu, but everyone in the betting shop where he worked called him George.

'Should I call you Adedayo, then?'

'No, you can call me George.'

We got into a conversation about betting. I wasn't much of a gambler, but Phil used to back the horses when we shared a flat in Earl's Court. He'd taught me the basics, so I could blag about singles, doubles, yankees and goliaths like a pro. It helped. Once he was on home ground, George talked twenty to the dozen. Sometimes unlucky punters ran amok towards the end of the afternoon and tried to smash the machines, he told me. Verbal abuse was common, violence against staff not unknown – on one occasion, someone had come in with a pickaxe. The shop had security screens to separate the staff from the clientele, but they didn't make him feel any safer.

I told him about my early days as a repo man, then described how the debt collecting industry had changed. Since I moved into management I didn't have to face threats of violence, I said, but I'd had my fair share of grief from debtors when I was treading the pavements. In retrospect, it was a mistake to tell George about the forced entries and doorstep brawls of my youth. They upset him more than I would have expected. He must have had a social conscience. It seemed strange for someone who worked in the gambling industry, but perhaps I seemed just as strange to him.

I raised the subject of murder by mentioning a drive-by shooting that had taken place in South Ockendon the previous week. George responded by telling me about gun crime in Port Harcourt. 'They have armed guards in the shopping malls,' he said. It meant that shoppers didn't have to keep looking over their shoulders, a necessity if they bought from open markets. But armed robbers still targeted the malls, and sometimes the Nigerian army was called in to deal with them.

'Do you mind if I ask you about the incident next door?' I said.

George looked surprised. 'What about it?'

'The gunshot,' I said. 'There was only one, wasn't there?'

'One shot.' George's voice had darkened. The murder still cast a long shadow, it seemed.

'How much could you hear?'

His eyes darted round the room. 'These walls are thin.'

'I know. I listen to Miss Prim's radio programmes all day long,' I said. 'Did you hear any shouting? Any raised voices?'

George hesitated, then shook his head.

'What did you hear?'

'Bang!' said George. He'd made a gun shape out of his hand, like a kid playing cops and robbers.

'You're sure it was a gun?' I said. 'Not someone kicking a ball against a garage door? Not a firework going off?'

'No, it was a gun. I have heard many guns.'

'What, around here?'

George shook his head. 'At home.'

'Oh, Port Harcourt,' I said. 'Did you hear anything after the shot?'

Beads of sweat appeared on George's forehead.

'Anything at all?'

He pulled off his baseball cap, took out a handkerchief and wiped his brow. He seemed to have lost his tongue. 'No,' he said at last.

'Did you see anyone? Running past the window, for instance?'

He continued to wipe his brow with the handkerchief.

'Can you remember what time you heard the shot?'

'I was getting ready for work,' he said, his voice almost a whisper.

I felt the muscles in my body tense. 'And when would that have been?'

George stared back at me defiantly. He didn't like where the conversation was taking him. He dropped his eyes and concentrated on folding his handkerchief into quarters. Getting the edges lined up seemed more important than talking to me. I wanted to say, 'Come on, George, I need the exact time. A hell of a lot depends on it.' But I didn't.

I waited as he patted the handkerchief flat and put it in his pocket. I was getting to know him better, my nervous neighbour. The last thing he wanted to talk about was the bloodbath next door. It was a pity that he'd chosen to settle in Johnson Terrace.

'Can you remember the time?' I repeated softly.

George thought about it. 'It could have been about a quarter to nine,' he said.

'A quarter to nine?' I couldn't stop myself yelling. My shout earned me a dirty look from George. He must have regretted opening his door to me. But if the gun had been fired at a quarter to nine instead of ten past eight—

'Are you sure?'

This time George left his handkerchief in his pocket and wiped the sweat off his brow with the palm of his hand. 'They let us in at five to nine,' he said, 'so I usually leave here at a quarter to. That's when I think I heard it. I stayed home that day.'

A quarter to nine – five minutes after Conrad's train had departed for Fenchurch Street! This was the breakthrough. The first piece of solid evidence that Conrad couldn't have killed his flatmate. Another piece of testimony that hadn't found its way to the courtroom. If the police had done their job, and the defence hadn't been half asleep, the case against Conrad could have been shot down in flames. I wondered how Ursula Jolliffe would feel when we confronted her with George.

'Did you tell the police?' I said.

I waited a long time for George's reply and didn't get one. But it was clear from the way he was avoiding my eyes that he hadn't. Maybe they'd never asked him. Maybe he'd clammed up on them. The latter was more likely, I thought. George could have had reasons of his own for keeping his head below the parapet. When Conrad was charged, the real killer would have felt as safe as houses.

But if George had come forward with evidence that gave Conrad his alibi back, the hunt for suspects would have begun again. And then the real killer might – just might—

Later, back in my flat, my excitement began to cool. I wondered how far we could rely on George when it came to the crunch. What he'd told me was gold dust, but would he agree to give evidence in an appeal against Conrad's conviction? He seemed no more likely to cooperate with us than Wes. I kicked myself – it was my own fault. I'd given him a grilling, too much of a grilling. I'd slipped into my old ways, behaved like a repo man.

And even if he did agree to give evidence, would he stand up to cross examination by counsel for the Crown? Somehow I didn't think so. I could see him in the witness box, his voice fading to a whisper, beads of sweat on his brow, doing his party trick with the hanky while the court lost patience with him. I had to face the facts – as far as clearing Conrad's name was concerned, George was a no-hoper.

I spent a long time trying to figure out what to do next. In the end, I came to the conclusion there was no way round it. I had to get Mrs Wilderman to reconsider her testimony, withdraw it if possible. The problem was, I couldn't quite see how.

8

'I thought you weren't coming,' Janet snapped.

She was waiting outside Fenchurch Street station, the only motionless figure in a seething mass of commuters. It was six o'clock the following evening. I'd phoned her after my meeting with George. As before, I'd got her voicemail, so I left her a message about when he thought he'd heard the shot. This time Janet phoned back within minutes and suggested a meeting to talk things over. I jumped at the chance. It was easy for her to get to Fenchurch Street from where she lived, she said.

I hurried up to her and apologised for keeping her waiting, even though I was on time. She was wearing the same clothes as the day she'd stopped me in the street, a long navy coat and a red beret, but her cheeks had a sucked-in look and she wasn't wearing lipstick. Her grief was palpable.

'Let's find somewhere we can sit down,' I said.

'I'm not standing here any longer,' was the reply.

We walked off in search of a café.

'How are you feeling?' I asked.

'Like shit.'

There was nothing I could say to that.

'What do you think it's like,' she said, rounding on me, 'being alive when the person you loved more than anyone in the world has killed themselves?'

I tried to take her arm, but she pulled it away. 'I hate living.'

After that, neither of us spoke until we came to a café. 'Is this one all right?' I said.

Janet looked inside and wrinkled her nose. It was crowded with office workers. 'Why don't you come back?' she said.

'Come back?'

'Back to mine. It's not far.'

I wondered if I had the right to intrude on her grief, but she insisted. We travelled by Underground to Kilburn station. After exiting, we walked a couple of hundred yards until we came to a modern five-storey building, Aveley House. Janet's flat was on the top floor, number 507. She opened her front door on a tiny hallway that led to an equally tiny living room. There wasn't much in it, a small sofa, a coffee table and a TV in the corner.

For a few moments we stood there looking at each other. The tragedy in this woman's life would have brought anybody to their knees. It was surprising that she was prepared to talk to me. I felt bad about using her like that. But she was a crucial source for the book, and there was no way Clarissa was going to get her hands on my pension.

'Do you want a drink?' Janet said.

'Don't mind if I do.'

'Whisky OK?'

'Whisky will do nicely.'

I looked round the living room while Janet disappeared into the kitchen. Everything was neat and tidy, what there was of it. The fitted carpet was white, the same as the sofa, and both were spotless.

Janet reappeared with a bottle of whisky in one hand and two glasses in the other, gripping them expertly between her fingers. It made me wonder if she'd ever worked in a bar. She poured a generous amount into one of the glasses with a dexterity that impressed me.

'Do you want anything in it?'

'It's fine as it is.'

She poured herself a smaller one, sat beside me on the sofa and placed the bottle on the coffee table in front of us. Neither of us spoke. I was thinking of Conrad alone in his holding cell, looking at a sentence of life imprisonment, then reaching out for the only means of escape. Janet, I was sure of it, was thinking the same.

'Words can't describe how bad I feel about your brother,' I said. 'But we could at least try to clear his name. There's always the possibility of overturning the conviction posthumously. It'll mean lawyers, and lots of waiting, but it's been done before. If that's what you want, I'm willing to give it a go.'

Janet didn't reply.

'I'm more than willing,' I said. 'I'm all fired up. If that's what you want.'

'I suppose so,' she said without much enthusiasm.

'If we're going to do it,' I said, 'we need to discuss how to take things forward.'

'Take things forward?' There was more than a hint of petulance in her voice.

Perhaps I should have left it at that. But I was so glad she'd contacted me that I went straight ahead. 'There's a shedload of details to clear up before we can go to the lawyers,' I said.

'Details?'

'One thing I didn't understand about Conrad's trip to Colchester,' I said, 'was his reason for wanting to visit Wes. He hadn't seen him for years, so why would he want to visit him then?'

I was hoping Janet would have something to tell me. Conrad must have discussed it with her. But she kept her lips tightly shut. She was hurting badly, I could tell.

'I suppose you don't want to talk about it,' I said, 'but I think it was because Doug was planning a move to London. That would have left Conrad on his own. It would have been natural, wouldn't it, to reach out to someone else?'

Janet said nothing.

'But why Wes?'

She still didn't answer me. It was hard work. But if we wanted to convince the courts that Conrad was wrongfully convicted, we'd need to provide an explanation for every move he made. Otherwise, they'd fall back on Jolliffe's version of events and the appeal would fail.

'I'm surprised how easy it is to undermine the prosecution case,' I said, trying to encourage Janet to open up.

'If it's that easy,' she flashed back, 'why was my brother convicted?'

My heart sank. I felt that she was blaming me for failing to persuade my fellow jurors to change their minds. I was more than ready to defend myself. 'The police investigation was a disgrace,' I said. 'So was the prosecution. But the jury were the worst of the lot. They refused to do what they were supposed to do. Jolliffe's attack on your brother's character brought about a lynch-mob mentality. After that, it was guilty, guilty, guilty every step of the way. We were supposed to examine the evidence. But the other members of the jury wouldn't do that. Wait a minute, I said, let's take a critical look at what this witness said, let's assess the reliability of that witness, let's weigh everything in the balance. I argued and argued. But no one listened.'

Janet took a sip of whisky.

'I held out as long as I could,' I said.

I waited for her to say something. I waited a long time.

'There's a lot more I could tell you,' I said. 'Jury service was an eye-opener for me. It proved that the system can convict an innocent man on the flimsiest of evidence. On no evidence at all, actually.'

I was beginning to think I was wasting my time. I'd

done what she'd asked of me, more than she had a right to expect from a complete stranger. But that was before her brother killed himself. Since then everything had changed.

'What are you thinking?' I asked.

'Oh, nothing.'

'Nothing?'

'That jury wasn't up to much,' she said. 'That's what I was thinking.'

'They were terrible.'

'I thought you were vetted,' she said. 'Or trained or something.'

'No, they put us in the jury room and left us to it. Vetted? If that lot had been vetted, they wouldn't have been allowed to judge a dog show.'

Janet kicked off her shoes, stuck out her legs and wiggled her toes as if her feet were hurting. 'Tell me about it.'

That was better. 'The foreman was an idiot called Stan Tuffin,' I said. 'I don't think he'd ever chaired a meeting in his life. Or made a decision.'

'Oh,' said Janet. 'One of those.'

I told her how he'd called a vote before we'd been through the evidence. Even though the judge had told us to examine the evidence first.

'So how come the judge made him the foreman?'

'She didn't,' I said. 'We had to elect one ourselves. I suggested getting everybody to say what experience they'd had – chairing meetings, serving on other juries, things like that. So that we could make an informed decision.

But Stan had been scribbling in a little black book all through the trial, and it had impressed one of my fellow jurors. "You've taken tons of notes," she said to him, "so it ought to be you." Stan said, "OK then," and that's how he was appointed.'

'I don't like hearing that.'

'You'll like this even less,' I said, and told her about the self-employed plumber who wanted our deliberations over and done with as soon as possible. 'He was worried about losing customers. Understandable in a way, but not when a man's freedom is at stake. He was in business with his brother, so his application to be excused jury service was refused. They said his brother could carry on the business without him. But there was too much for his brother to manage on his own – customers were going elsewhere, he said. He was the one who leaned on Stan to call the vote. And Stan was too weak to say no. I objected, but I was overruled. We found Conrad guilty without giving the evidence the going-over it needed.'

If I'd been Janet I wouldn't have wanted to hear another word about that jury. It would have depressed me. But it seemed to have lifted her spirits. She leaned forward, put her drink on the coffee table and got out her phone. 'What did you say his name was? That plumber?'

I told her.

She googled and found his website. 'That's one plumber I won't be phoning if I get a burst pipe,' she said. The change of mood surprised me. The dark clouds were drifting away. 'Anything else?' she asked.

'I think I've said enough.' I was sure that plenty of

juries perform their duties conscientiously. Perhaps most of them do. But the system doesn't guarantee it. You only have to include people like Stan Tuffin and the plumber and things can go badly wrong.

'You're a mystery to me,' Janet said. 'My brother gets convicted by a rubbish jury but there's one shining exception among them. Someone who pops up from nowhere like a fairy godmother.'

'I've never been called that before.'

She twisted round on the sofa to look at me. 'Why do you care so much about Conrad? Someone you never knew. Why do you want to clear his name? If you do prove him innocent, the authorities won't thank you for it. There will be a fuss and you could be accused of troublemaking. Bringing the law into disrepute, or whatever they call it. Aren't you scared?'

I didn't answer. I had no worries about bringing the law into disrepute. As far as my family was concerned, the law had brought itself into disrepute when it convicted my father. A teenage pupil had accused him of inappropriate touching and it had ended his career. No matter that there were no witnesses. No matter that the pupil had a reputation for dishonesty. No matter that my father had disciplined him for scratching another pupil's initials on a laboratory worktop. The allegation had been enough. It was an allegation of child abuse, and juries, we were told, are extremely unwilling to acquit in such cases.

'Yes, I think you are scared,' Janet said. 'And I've got a feeling you're going to chicken out.'

The accusation stung. 'I sat on a jury that made a bad decision,' I said, 'and I can't live with it. Most people never imagine that a jury can get things so wrong—'

'So you want to make amends.'

I took a deep breath. 'If I can prove that Conrad was innocent, it would give the criminal justice system the bloody nose it deserves.'

'You've certainly been trying hard enough.'

'If only more people were prepared to speak out,' I said.

Janet pecked me on the cheek, got up from the sofa and walked to the other side of the room. She leaned against the wall next to the TV, looking at me thoughtfully as she swirled the whisky in her glass. I got the impression she was trying to decide if I was being straight with her.

'I admire you, Tony,' she said. 'I admired you from the moment I met you. Even before that. I saw the disgust on your face when the foreman announced the verdict. It was an honest face, and that's something I can look up to.'

'I admire you too, Janet. It takes courage to fight for your brother's good name.'

We both laughed.

'Tell me about yourself,' she said. 'Tell me why you're so different.'

'I'm not different. I'm ordinary. I work in an office. I was called for jury service. That's about it.'

It seemed to satisfy her. 'So what do you think we should do next?' she said.

At last we were getting somewhere. I jumped straight in. 'Let's focus on the time of the gunshot,' I said. 'Do you remember Mrs Wilderman's performance in the witness box? The librarian who said she was walking her dog past the flat? She didn't sound at all sure about the time she heard the gun go off. But as I said over the phone, my neighbour was convinced he heard it much later, when Conrad was on the train. It might be useful if you went along and had a word with Mrs Wilderman—' I stopped because of the expression on Janet's face.

'Me? Have a word with *who?*'

'Mrs Wilderman,' I said. 'She might admit she could have been mistaken. She might say that ten past eight was only a guess. She might even change her mind—'

'Why me?'

'Because you're Conrad's sister,' I said. 'Mrs Wilderman is more likely to listen if it's a relative doing the asking. That way, she'll realise the effect her evidence has had on Conrad's family. And you're a woman. She's more likely to talk to another woman than to me. If she had the slightest doubt about the time, she'll want to share it with you. If only to ease her conscience. I've been thinking—'

'For God's sake, Tony, shut it.'

Janet's outburst stopped me in full flight. I'd said the wrong thing, but for the life of me I couldn't see how.

'I thought you wanted to help,' she said.

'But help is what I'm trying to do.'

'Is that what you call it? Chatting to the neighbours? Is that it?'

'Talking to the neighbours could get Conrad a pardon,' I said.

'And what use would that be?' she demanded.

'Pardons are words. They won't bring him back, will they? All you're doing is messing about.' Tears had appeared on her cheeks. 'You're no use, Tony. You're letting me down.'

'That's not fair,' I said. 'I've found one – no, two witnesses the defence overlooked, and I've knocked a hole in the evidence of a third.'

I thought Janet was going to throw her glass at me. 'You haven't found out anything worth knowing, not a thing,' she said, shaking with anger. 'I could have told you that Conrad had made an arrangement to go to Colchester. I could have told you that he worshipped Doug.'

There was no way we could have a sensible conversation while she was behaving like this. 'Why don't you go and lie down?' I said, swallowing the last of my whisky. I got up from the sofa and headed for the door. 'Try to get a good night's sleep. I'll give you a call tomorrow.'

'You'll have to do better than this if you really want to help,' she shouted at me.

'Janet—'

'I'll tell you how you can help,' she raged. 'Find the man who killed Doug. Get him for me. Forget the time people heard the gun go off. Forget the times of trains. I want you to get the man who did it. I want him to know what it's like to be locked in a cell for the rest of his life. And I hope he hangs himself when he's in there.'

9

I'd never known anyone as eaten up with grief as Janet Connor. She was after revenge, and I didn't blame her. It was only when I got home that I realised what I'd taken on. The last thing I'd said before I left was, 'OK, I'll do it. I'll find the man who killed Doug.' I'd said it to calm her down. I was worried that she might do something stupid. But now, in the relative quiet of my flat, I had time to reconsider. Track down a murderer?

When we first met, Janet had told me that Doug had been killed by a dealer. She hadn't given a reason. She seemed to base it on her knowledge, or maybe no more than her assumption, that Doug was doing drugs. That didn't fit with painting pretty pictures of carnations, but it was plausible. What was puzzling was why Janet had seemed so sure. Anyone could have killed Doug. It could have been a burglar, although there were no signs of a break-in – one of the things that had counted against Conrad. And the killer might not have been local. He could have come from miles away.

The sensible thing would have been to forget Janet and her unrealistic expectations. But we needed her for the book. Phil had told his agent that Conrad's sister was cooperating with me. She was supplying me with exclusive information, he'd said, exaggerating in the way he usually does. That had been the game-changer. It was what had persuaded his agent to give us the go-ahead.

So that night I phoned Phil in Hollywood. If I went looking for the murderer, it would alter the nature of the book we were writing. A wrongful conviction story would become a whodunit. I needed to check it out with him.

Phil answered the phone sounding chipper. 'I'm staying with a film producer,' he said, 'in his delightful urban oasis a stone's throw from the Cahuenga Corridor.'

The dull roar of a jet could be heard passing overhead. I imagined Phil lounging on a sunny terrace, under a pergola or wherever the rich go to chill out in California. He didn't have to tell me about it. I could see the palm trees, the sunloungers, the light shimmering on the surface of the pool. And the cool drink close at hand. I didn't waste time asking what the Cahuenga Corridor was. I gave it to him straight about the holes I'd picked in the prosecution case.

'To be honest,' he said, 'I didn't think you'd get the project off the ground. But here you are, reporting back to me already. And it's solid stuff you're telling me. I'm beginning to believe that you were right. Maybe Conrad wasn't the killer. I like it.'

'And I've met with Janet,' I said.

Phil liked that even more. 'We need the voice of someone who knew Conrad personally,' he said. 'Get her childhood memories next time you see her. Donkey rides on the beach, what their dad did for a living, that sort of thing. Keep in touch with her, and see if you can get some family photos off her too.'

I moved to the point of the call. 'How about going after the murderer? The man who really did kill Doug? Rubbishing the prosecution case is a yawn. Finding the man who did it would be a story.'

Phil didn't respond at first. 'You? Find the killer?' he said eventually. 'Isn't that a bit ... presumptuous?'

'Forget human interest,' I said. 'If we want a bestseller, we'll have to pin the crime on someone other than Conrad. That's the only solid proof he didn't do it.'

Phil laughed. 'Look here, Tony, it's not feasible. A juryman blows the whistle on a false conviction – that's you. That's within your comfort zone. But to think you can *solve the crime*, take on the role of *investigator*—'

'It's what Janet wants,' I said. 'I don't think she'll go along with us for less.'

'Really?'

I told him how Janet had kicked off. I told him she'd have nothing more to do with us if we didn't give her what she wanted. I reminded him that I was living yards from where the murder took place. I was picking up details the police had missed – or wanted to bury. I had crucial contacts – Arthur Drury, Len Mackle, Miss Prim – after only a few days on the job.

'Tell me,' I said. 'Can you have a murder story without a murderer?'

There was another silence. This time it was followed by an even bigger laugh. 'You're telling me my job,' Phil said. 'No, I don't suppose you can. Hold the line, I'll trail it in front of Joseph. He knows the markets better than anyone.'

There was a clunk as Phil put down his phone. I didn't have to wait long before he was back.

'Tony? You still there?'

'What's the score?' I said.

He sounded ashamed for doubting me. 'Joseph didn't have to think twice. He says find the killer.'

It was easy to say. But after sleeping on it, I woke the next morning wondering if I'd been carried away by my own optimism. I didn't have much holiday left. Just a few weeks to find someone who hated Doug enough to kill him. Someone who had no qualms about setting Conrad up for a crime he did not commit.

I smiled to myself when I realised that I'd undertaken something I'd told Janet I lacked the knowledge and the skills for. But I didn't have much choice in the matter. I had to make the project work. It was partly because I didn't want to let Phil down. He'd committed himself to his agent, and I could guess how awkward it would be if I left him in the lurch. The thought of the money was a big pull, too. A bigger pull, the more I thought about it.

As I had no idea where to start, I resurrected the plan to interview Mrs Wilderman. If Janet didn't feel up to it, I'd take it on myself. At the trial, Mrs Wilderman had been described as a senior librarian in charge of the local history archives at a public library. Which public library wasn't stated, but it was reasonable to assume it was not far from Riverwell. A quick search on the internet established that yes, Riverwell did possess a public library. A follow up phone call confirmed that there was a Mrs Wilderman on the staff. I asked what materials were kept there, and it turned out that Mrs Wilderman had a special interest in maps and aerial photographs of the area. All I had to do was invent an interest in local history, and a reason for wanting to consult some old maps. I did that on my way there.

Riverwell Public Library was a red brick Edwardian building, set back from the high street in a little square. I was approaching the impressive stone entrance when my phone rang.

'Tony, it's Janet.'

That was quite a surprise. 'Are you OK?' I asked.

'But are you?' she replied.

'Why, yes,' I said, 'I'm fine. It's you I'm worried about. You didn't sound OK last night.'

'But I am. Oh no Tony, I'm not. I'm phoning to apologise. I'm ashamed of the way I treated you. All that shouting and screaming – if it didn't put you off me for ever, I don't know what would.'

'Don't worry about it.'

'But I am worried about it. I treated you disgracefully. All the work you've done to clear Conrad's name, and I wasn't the least bit grateful. And the nasty things I said to you. They were so cruel. I didn't mean them. But my mind is full of Conrad every minute of the day and night. I can't think of anybody else. Oh Tony, it's so much worse at night. I can see Conrad in the darkness – actually see him alone in his cell. Can you believe it? And what he did to himself – can you imagine the state of mind he must have been in? To – to do something like *that*?'

'I understand,' I said. 'You've been through hell.'

'What I said last night was true.' Her voice was thick with emotion. 'I like you – I like you more every time we meet. I want us to go on seeing each other. But—'

'Let's put last night behind us,' I said. 'Let's concentrate on what has to be done. Do you still want me to look for the killer?'

'Yes, I do. And there's something else,' she said.

'Oh?'

'I've been talking to someone who might help us.'

'Help how?'

'A man phoned. He said he has something to tell me. It's a bit complicated, but he said it was something I needed to know. It's about the murder.'

'Do you think he's genuine?' I said. 'There are a lot of disturbed people out there.'

'I know. If you heard some of the things the neighbours have been saying about our family—'

'You don't have to tell me,' I said. I was remembering

the torrent of filth that followed my father's conviction. 'Did this person give his name?'

'Bear with me.' There was a rustle of paper. 'His name is … is … I've got it here. Mr Brayne hyphen Thompson. B-R-A-Y-N-E. Double-barrelled.'

'And what has he got to say?'

Janet hesitated. 'Tony, I'm frightened. I haven't been able to sleep since … you know. It feels like there's someone in my bedroom, someone who wants to harm me. I keep the light on. It's been preying on my mind. I don't seem capable of thinking straight any more.'

'What does this person know that's so important,' I said, 'this Mr—?'

'Brayne-Thompson. He wouldn't say over the phone. He wants to meet me. He gave me an address. It's a hotel not far from where I live.'

'A hotel! You don't intend turning up, do you? Mr Brayne-Thompson sounds a bit of a weirdo.'

Janet didn't answer me. But I could tell she was still on the line.

'You'll have to be careful,' I said. 'Why has he come to you now?'

Janet gave a deep sigh. 'He said he knew a relative of mine. He recognised our name on the news.'

'Why hasn't he gone to the police?'

'I don't know. Maybe he'll explain when I meet him.'

'When's that?'

'Tonight at seven o'clock.'

I nearly exploded. 'Don't go.'

'I have to.'

I thought it over. 'OK, but you're not going on your own. I'll come with you.'

There was a gasp of relief. 'Bless you, Tony, bless you.'

'No problem,' I said. 'Which hotel is it?'

'The Brookmyre. Ten minutes from where I live, if you go by car.'

'I'll pick you up outside your flat at a quarter to seven.'

'I knew I could rely on you, Tony. You're my rock.'

Abandoning the plan to talk to Mrs Wilderman, I turned on my heel and walked back to Johnson Terrace. I had always found history boring anyway.

10

When I drew up outside Aveley House, the lipstick was back on but there were still signs of strain on Janet's face. I hoped that our meeting with Mr Brayne-Thompson wouldn't pile any more pressure on her. She was close to the edge as it was.

I opened the passenger door and in she jumped. Pulling away from the kerb, I followed her instructions and drove further down the road. We passed a park, half a mile of flat conversions and a row of shops. At a crossroads I said, 'Where to?'

'Keep straight ahead.'

A few minutes later she said, 'Turn left here,' so I took a left into a pleasant tree-lined road of semis. At the bottom we came to a T-junction with a tall glass-and-concrete building opposite. A sign said *Brookmyre Hotel*. None of the flagpoles along the front had a flag on it, but there was a decent-sized car park behind them. I drove in and parked.

'You lead the way,' Janet said. She sounded nervous.

We entered the lobby. The décor was commercial-anonymous, a mixture of black granite surfaces, low ceilings and subdued lighting. It was the kind of venue companies use for motivational conferences, not the kind you'd choose for a relaxing holiday. Janet told the young woman at reception that we had a meeting with Mr Brayne-Thompson. The young woman looked at her computer screen.

'Mr Brayne-Thompson is waiting for you in the Callaghan Room,' she said, pointing to swing doors on the other side of the lobby.

The swing doors opened on a large lounge with a grand piano at the far end. It was laid out with high-backed armchairs and coffee tables. The only person in sight was a middle-aged man sitting at one of the tables. He stood up to greet us as we approached.

Dressed in a dark brown three piece suit, his wrinkled skin and downturned mouth put me in mind of a tortoise. The reptilian effect was increased by the half-moon glasses perched partway down his nose.

'You must be Ms Connor,' he said to Janet.

'Yes, and this is my friend Mr Quirke,' she replied.

'Kenneth Brayne-Thompson,' he said and shook hands with each of us in turn. He seemed genuine, but I decided to defer judgement until I'd heard what he had to say.

A waiter appeared from nowhere to take our orders. Brayne-Thompson had a glass of whisky in front of him.

I asked him if he'd like another. Thanking me in clipped tones he asked for a Glenlivet. I ordered a double for him and coffees for Janet and me.

'Well,' I said, 'here we all are.'

'We haven't met,' Brayne-Thompson said, looking at me. 'Perhaps I should mention that I'm a psychotherapist in private practice.'

'And you've something to tell us?' said Janet.

'You must understand,' he said, 'that I shouldn't be talking to you at all. There are issues of professional confidentiality.' He looked at the door as if he was thinking of going back on his offer. I was half-expecting him to walk out, but he must have decided we were worth it.

'I have a client,' he said, 'a gentleman I've been seeing for more than a year now, someone who developed an interest in the Connor trial. A rather unhealthy interest, if the truth be known.'

'Unhealthy?' I queried, but Brayne-Thompson ignored me.

'To get straight to the point,' he said, 'this client has led me to suspect that he was involved in the murder of Douglas Hamilton. He could be a fantasist, of course, but as his therapist I'm not inclined to take that view.'

'Involved in the murder?' I said. 'That's quite a claim. What makes you so sure?'

Brayne-Thompson looked at me over his half-moon glasses. 'Perhaps I should explain the arrangement I have with my clients,' he said. 'They're free to telephone me at any time of the day or night if they need my help. That's what happened the day Mr Connor went on trial. It was all over the news, of course, so I knew what my client was talking about.'

'Go on,' said Janet.

'This gentleman,' Brayne-Thompson said, 'let's call him Mr A, rang me around twelve o'clock that night and stayed on the line for more than an hour. He was very upset. He wouldn't tell me what the matter was, but it sounded serious. If I'd thought there was any chance of him self-harming, I would have alerted the community psychiatric team. But I knew Mr A very well, and I felt confident there wasn't much risk of that. So I arranged to see him in my consulting room. In the early hours of the morning, you understand. I would have done the same for any client who phoned me in similar circumstances.'

The waiter arrived with our drinks.

'This gentleman,' Janet said when we were alone again, 'what exactly did he say?' She was leaning forward in her seat, as if scared of missing something.

'It's not as simple as that,' Brayne-Thompson said. 'It's more a matter of what he didn't say.' He took a sip of whisky and paused for a few moments to savour it. 'I was shocked when I unlocked my consulting room door to let him in. Mr A prides himself on his appearance, but that night his hair – oh, my goodness. Usually he wears it in a quiff, like an old-fashioned rock 'n' roll star. That night his hair was a mess. And there were food stains down the front of his shirt. He stank of sweat and wasn't wearing any of the silver jewellery he usually has on. And his eyes

– he looked haunted, that's all I can say. They were deep in their sockets, which is always a sign.

'"You've taken something," I said to him, "and it may have been contaminated. Let's get you to hospital and they can pump you out."

'He denied taking anything. Not for the last twelve hours, at least. No, he said, he was hearing a voice and he was terrified.'

'I'm sorry to interrupt,' I said, 'but would you mind telling us your client's name? It is rather important.'

'I'm bound by a professional code of conduct,' Brayne-Thompson said, rather preciously I thought. 'I may have said too much already. I'm risking my livelihood by talking to you at all.'

Janet must have thought I was going to turn our informant against us. 'That's all right, Mr Brayne-Thompson,' she said. 'I'm grateful that you contacted me. You don't have to say any more than you want.'

'Well,' he said, giving her a little nod of appreciation, 'I'll try to be brief. The consultation ended without Mr A telling me what the voice was saying. But it was clear that it was disturbing him.

'Before the Connor trial, I'd been seeing him fortnightly. After that first call, he telephoned me almost every night. It was always late, often after midnight. Long, rambling, incoherent speeches. I won't trouble you with everything he said. But I soon began to suspect that he'd had something to do with the murder. It was because of what he kept saying: "That was my gun." Over and over, "That was my gun."'

'What gun?' I said.

Brayne-Thompson sent an irritated glance in my direction. 'My client was very upset when the media reported the discovery of the murder weapon,' he said. 'That was the gun he was referring to. But to me, his meaning was clear. He was confessing. Confessing that he'd been involved in the murder.'

'It doesn't sound like a confession to me,' I said.

'I haven't practised psychotherapy for twenty-five years without recognising a confession when I hear one,' Brayne-Thompson replied. 'Confessions often come in disorganised, incoherent fragments. The perpetrator feels a need to get the wrong-doing off his chest. He can't contain his secret any longer. But he feels ashamed of what he's done, and that prevents him from admitting his guilt. The result is the mental turmoil I witnessed in Mr A. It's a fight to the death between the urge to relieve feelings of guilt and the need to avoid the self-loathing that full disclosure would entail.'

The psychobabble was beginning to irritate me. I risked Janet's displeasure again by asking a blunt question. 'Why haven't you reported this to the police?'

'I have enough knowledge of the law to realise that it wouldn't count as evidence,' Brayne-Thompson said. 'Nothing Mr A told me would be admissible in court – nothing that a half-decent barrister couldn't explain away in a couple of minutes.

'But to cut to the chase. I decided to lead him on, hoping he would say something more substantial. Perhaps he'd mention some detail about the crime that hadn't been reported in the media, something that only the murderer would know.'

'And did he?'

'I listened to him for hours on end, most nights of the trial,' Brayne-Thompson said. 'Phone call by phone call we inched closer to what I was hoping to hear. And eventually we got there. He told me he had known Mr Hamilton personally.'

'Personally? How personally?' I said. 'I'm sorry to keep insisting on clarification, Mr Brayne-Thompson, but there's a lot hanging on this, you know.'

Brayne-Thompson gave a little smile. 'I haven't mentioned it yet, but my client has a chequered history. He is known to the police. To put it bluntly, he's a cocaine dealer. And he was supplying Douglas Hamilton with illegal substances.'

I looked at Janet. She was drinking in everything Brayne-Thompson said.

'Mr A was very agitated the day the verdict was announced,' he continued. 'So I asked him, "Do you feel bad about what you've done to Conrad Connor? Because he didn't do that murder, did he?" Mr A didn't answer. So I said, "Do you feel bad about what you did to Douglas Hamilton?" His reply chilled me to the bone. "I'd had all I could stand from Hamilton. Nobody treats me like that."

'"I'm talking about that Saturday morning at Johnson Terrace," I said. "Do you feel sorry about it now?"

'My client did not answer. But I could sense he wanted to get something off his chest, so I got straight to the point. "You killed Douglas Hamilton, didn't you?" I said.

'This made him very angry. "What I do is my affair," he shouted down the phone. "I don't owe you a thing. You are a madman."

'"I think you did it," I said.

'"Did what?"

'"Kill Douglas Hamilton."

'My client laughed. "No one will believe you," he said. "There isn't any evidence."'

Brayne-Thompson sat back in his chair and took another sip of whisky. I met his eyes over the top of his half-moon glasses. They were drilling into me, trying to judge my reaction.

'Did he say any more?' Janet asked.

'Indeed he did,' Brayne-Thompson replied. 'He said things like, "Why are you going on and on at me?" and "I wish you'd shut your trap." I was glad it was only a phone call. If he'd been in my consulting room, I would have been worried for my safety. My client was furious. "You think you know what happened to Hamilton?" he shouted. "Well, you're wrong. No one will believe a word you say." And then he rang off. I haven't heard from him since.'

Brayne-Thompson threw the remains of the whisky down his throat and looked at his watch.

'So who is your client?' I said.

'You must agree to keep my name out of this. And never to contact me again.'

'In that case, what you've told us doesn't help. It would only be credible coming from you.'

Janet grabbed my arm. 'No. I give you my word,

Mr Brayne-Thompson, that we will never mention your name to anybody. Or contact you again.'

'Is that agreed, Mr… um…' Brayne-Thompson said.

'Quirke,' I said, and looked at Janet. Her eyes were pleading with me. 'Yes,' I said to Brayne-Thompson with some reluctance. 'It's agreed.'

Janet gave my arm a squeeze.

'Vilday,' Brayne-Thompson said. 'My client is a gentleman called Gregory Vilday. He doesn't live very far from where the murder took place.' He paused. 'In the village of Mowbridge, number 9 Church Lane. But if you tell anybody I've given you his name and address, anybody at all, I shall lodge a complaint with the police. I shall say you've been harassing me and I shall press charges. I shall say you are mentally unbalanced. If you try to involve me in any way whatsoever, I shall sue you.'

He was already on his feet when he said this. I stood to shake hands, but he walked off without so much as a goodbye. My eyes never left his short, ungainly figure as he threaded a path between the coffee tables towards the exit. When he reached the swing doors he stopped, looked back at us for a few moments, then disappeared.

'Psychotherapist, is he?' I said to Janet. 'I still don't understand why he contacted you instead of the police. And I don't buy what he said about professional confidentiality. That doesn't apply when someone has committed a crime. It was his responsibility to report it.'

'Maybe he was too scared of the consequences,' Janet said. 'But he thinks that someone ought to know.'

'He knew your family, you said?'

'A cousin of mine was in the forces. I was aware he'd had therapy, but I never knew who'd treated him. I didn't know it was Mr Brayne-Thompson. Not until he got in touch with me.'

'When was that?'

Janet didn't give me an answer and I didn't insist on one. I was convinced that Brayne-Thompson had contacted her some time ago, probably immediately after the trial. I thought back to the first time Janet and I met. *I know who it was*, she'd said, and then she'd backed off. She hadn't wanted to tell me about Vilday then, I suspected, because she hadn't been sure of me. Well, I said to myself, she can be sure of me now.

'Let's see who he is,' I said, got out my phone and googled Brayne-Thompson, psychotherapist.

> ## WELCOME TO KENNETH BRAYNE-THOMPSON ONLINE
> *Counsellor/Psychotherapist*
> *Counselling/psychotherapy for individuals, couples, groups. I specialise in couple and relationship counselling, anger management, post-traumatic stress and self-esteem/confidence-building.*

There was even a photo. It made him look younger than the business-suited tortoise we'd been talking to, but there was no doubt that our informant was who he said he was.

'So there it is,' I said to Janet. 'We'll have to accept him at face value.'

'I knew it was going to be a dealer,' she said.

11

All attention now focused on Gregory Vilday. My first step was to drop in at the Swan the following day. I pushed through the door to find a pasty-faced youth polishing glasses behind the bar. It was the mid-morning lull.

'Is Len in today?' I asked as he pulled my pint.

The youth frowned as if he didn't know whether he was allowed to tell me. 'In the cellar,' he said.

'I need a word with him. All right if I go down?'

The youth let me behind the bar. I carried my pint down to the cellar and found Len bent over a barrel, bottom towards me. He was doing something clever with a length of plastic tubing. A jug on a wooden stool beside him was half-full of foamy brew.

'Hate to bother you, Len,' I said, 'but have you heard of someone called Gregory Vilday?'

'Oh, it's you,' he said without looking round. 'Why the sudden interest in Mr Vilday?'

I'd decided to be open with him. If I wanted Len to be open with me, there wasn't any sense in holding back. 'There's a rumour he did the Hamilton shooting,' I said. 'I was hoping you could tell me something about him.'

Len stopped what he was doing, straightened up and turned to face me. He had to keep his head down because of the low beams. It made him look more alarmed than he probably was. 'You don't want anything to do with Vilday,' he said. 'I'd rather get into a cage with a tiger.'

'One day our paths may cross,' I said. 'I'd be grateful for anything you can tell me about him. Nice pint, by the way.' I took a sip.

'Let's go upstairs,' Len said, 'and talk in comfort.' He made his way to the cellar steps, brushing against a dangling light bulb as he went. It swung wildly, sending long shadows racing round the cobwebby vault. I followed him up the steps, careful not to spill my pint.

The youth behind the bar was still polishing glasses.

'Give me a pale ale, Billy,' Len said and led me to a seat in a corner.

'So that's the latest, is it?' he said. 'Vilday did the Drury Towers job?'

'It's what people are saying. I've never been convinced it was Connor. I'm looking for dirt on Vilday, if you've got any.'

'Solving murder cases now?' Len said.

Billy brought his pale ale to our table.

'You could call it my latest hobby,' I said.

'I hope you're not going to stir up any trouble. Most people round here think Connor got what was coming to him.'

'You always gave me the impression you had doubts about the verdict,' I said.

Len shifted uneasily in his seat. 'In the interests of peace and quiet, I keep them to myself.' He took a sip of pale ale. 'But I'll say this. I could never have imagined Conrad Connor with a gun. He wouldn't have known which end to hold.'

'Are you serious?'

'If he did what they said, he wouldn't have done it with a gun. There's a lot of people who'll never touch one, let alone use it. The lads used to come in here from time to time and Connor always seemed that way himself. It surprised me when I heard. He must have had a side to him I never knew. Up to then, I was convinced he would never have hurt a fly.'

'So you think it could have been Vilday?'

'I'm not saying it was, I'm not saying it wasn't.'

'If there's anything you can tell me about him,' I said, 'I'm all ears.'

'There isn't much,' Len replied. But there was. According to Len, Vilday began his criminal career in his late teens and was sent to prison for extortion. He came out a year later initiated into crack and cocaine dealing. After that he worked the clubs. The closest he got to being locked up a second time was when he was charged with rape. The case went as far as the Crown Court, but he was acquitted. There were rumours about the intimidation of witnesses, but Len didn't know the details.

'And that's about it,' he said.

It was a good start. I took the opportunity to ask something else while I had Len's undivided attention. 'Where could a man get hold of an illegal firearm around here?'

Len looked so shocked I hastened to explain. 'No one has ever connected Conrad to the murder weapon,' I said. 'I'm working on the idea that it was Vilday's. He must have got it from somewhere. I'd like to talk to a few dealers in unlicensed weapons, if I can find any. It might be difficult to make the connection, but it's worth a try.'

Len gave a nervous laugh. 'Why are you asking me?'

'Come on, Len, you know everything that's going on in Riverwell.'

He frowned. 'There's a trade in illegal weaponry, I do know that. A lot of it takes place in the pubs. But if I thought anyone was selling guns in the Swan, he'd be out on his ear in two seconds flat.'

'I wasn't thinking of the Swan. I was thinking generally.'

Len took another sip of pale ale. 'You must be mad if you want to start playing that game.'

'I'm after leads, that's all.'

Len was looking uncomfortable. I could see I'd gone too far. 'Another pale ale?' I said.

Len shook his head. He wanted to get back to his beloved cellar.

'Thanks for your help,' I said. I was just as happy to finish my drink and be on my way. At least I had a better picture of our chief suspect.

Mowbridge was a pretty little village about ten miles north of Riverwell. I was thinking of driving there in the hope of getting a closer look at Vilday, but an unexpected turn of events made that unnecessary.

It happened in the dead of night. Arthur Drury woke at one o'clock, struggling for breath. Then, in the words of the grief-stricken Ma, so distraught that she shared the experience with any tenant who would listen, 'with one great shudder, he was gone'. There was widespread sympathy in the local community. Arthur had been a popular character along Johnson Terrace – always cheerful, always ready to lend a helping hand. He was generous too. He often did odd jobs for local pensioners and didn't charge them.

If you wanted somewhere with plenty of parking to say your last farewells, the memorial lawn they chose for Arthur's cremation would be as good a place as any. I drove through the entrance gates at the regulation five miles per hour, parked my car and walked to the crematorium along a well-maintained gravel path. The chapel, with its white stuccoed walls, high roof and pointed windows, stood in a landscaped clump of firs like something out of a Disney cartoon.

I was surprised how many mourners had turned up. Most were middle-aged or older, some a lot older. There was much shaking of hands and hugging, as if they hadn't seen each other for years. The only person I recognised was Miss Prim, standing alone at the edge of the crowd, a long black shawl over her shoulders. She looked frailer than ever.

'I liked Arthur,' she said when I joined her. 'Not that I had much to do with him.' She pulled the shawl tight round her neck. 'I hope Ma's not going to sell up. I was talking to an estate agent I know— Oh my,' she interrupted herself, looking at the entrance gates. 'Here they come.'

I followed her gaze to a convoy of vehicles moving along the drive. The car in front was shiny and black, but it wasn't a hearse. Undertakers' limousines don't have blue lights on their roofs. The vehicle behind it was a prison van, easily identified by its mesh-covered windows. A regular patrol car brought up the rear.

'It's Jason,' said Miss Prim.

'Who's Jason?'

Miss Prim didn't answer me. Her eyes were following the vehicles as they described a half-circle in front of the chapel before coming to a halt. Two uniformed officers jumped out of the prison van, hurried to the rear and threw open the doors. A young man appeared in the doorway and the waiting mourners surged round. He was slightly built and dressed in a dark suit and black tie. With one wrist handcuffed to the officer behind him, his progress down the steps was awkward to say the least.

'Who's Jason?' I asked a second time.

'Jason Drury,' said Miss Prim. 'The Drurys' only son.'

He was quite a celebrity, it seemed. After the cuffs had

been removed the crowd pressed even closer. Men shook him by the hand. Women threw their arms around his neck and kissed him. He could have been a star of stage or screen. But he didn't react to any of it.

'The Drurys' son in prison?' I said, incredulous. 'What for?'

'Armed robbery,' Miss Prim said. 'Eighteen years, poor lad, and he hasn't got through the first one yet. Ma Drury's very worried about him.'

He seemed too young to be a violent offender, too child-like. 'If I had an armed robber in the family,' I said, 'I'd be worried too.'

Miss Prim frowned. 'It's not that,' she said. 'It's his state of mind. He can't do his time. He smashes up his cell, self-harms, all those sorts of things. Ma doesn't think he'll make it.'

'That's horrible.'

'Yes, it is,' she said. 'Poor little Jason's not like his dad.'

'Come again?'

Miss Prim pushed her glasses up her nose and looked at me quizzically. 'Didn't you know about Arthur?'

I shook my head.

'Arthur Drury did a twenty-year stretch and it didn't trouble him one jot. Built of boilerplate, our landlord. Late landlord, I should say, God rest his soul. He did those years as if it was a weekend. They gave him hell. Beatings, solitary confinement, bread and water, I don't know what. And in those days prisoners were three to a cell and had to slop out. On one occasion, he even bit his own finger off so they'd take him to hospital. He thought it would give him a better chance of escaping. Try anything, Arthur would. It didn't work out, because they chained him to his bed and he lost bags of remission. But none of it had any effect on him. He came out the same as he went in, people said. Smaller, of course – he'd shrunk – but it was the same old Arthur.

'Jason isn't like that. He was screaming to be let out after twenty-four hours. Crying for his mother. It's having a diabolical effect on Ma – she's very caring, you know, used to be a nurse. Trained at the London Hospital. Just her luck the men in her life have given her so much grief. Goodness knows why she married Arthur Drury. Fat lot of good it did her. More fool her, say I.'

I found it difficult to imagine the harmless old man who'd fixed the knocking pipe in number 12 as a convicted criminal. But it set me thinking. 'Was Arthur ever into drug dealing?' I said.

'Certainly not. Arthur was a specialist and proud of it. Safe-breaking. He went to prison for the Cain-Brunner gold robbery, you know.'

'You should have told me,' I said. 'I would have changed the lock on my door.'

Miss Prim gave me another disapproving look. 'You shouldn't jump to conclusions. He'd do anything for the tenants, Mr Drury would. A proper gentleman and courteous with it. When he came out of prison he decided to go straight. That's when they started the letting business. Talk about chutzpah. On the day of his release, Ma collected him from the prison gates in a horse-drawn carriage. That was to show the authorities how little they cared.'

We'd been so deep in conversation we hadn't noticed that the chapel doors were open. Jason, his jailers and the other mourners had gone inside. By the time Miss Prim and I joined them, the chapel was full and we had to squeeze ourselves on to the back pew. Jason was at the front, his jailers in the pew behind. His head was constantly on the move, staring at the vaulted roof one moment and the altar next, the windows one moment and the marble effect floor after that. He seemed confused by his surroundings. I supposed it was because they'd drugged him to the eyeballs.

I was still trying to make myself comfortable on the hard wooden seat when there was a crunch of wheels on the gravel outside. This was followed by the discreet slamming of car doors and the shuffling of feet in the vestibule. A few seconds later the cortège entered in grand style. Arthur Drury – gold robber, jailbird, caring landlord – was carried up the aisle on the shoulders of four solemn-faced pallbearers, followed by Ma Drury in a long black dress, floppy funeral hat and thick veil. A line of principal mourners trailed behind.

Jason didn't seem to notice his father's coffin when it was placed on the stand in front of him. He was too busy staring at the flowers on the window sills. He couldn't have seen many lilies where he spent his days now, certainly none arranged as tastefully as the ones laid on for his father.

I don't remember much about the service. My mind was working overtime, trying to get a handle on what Miss Prim had said about Arthur Drury. It had come as a shock. I now regarded the Drury family in a new light – Phil had been spot-on when he said the area was alive with criminals. They were popping up all around me. So when the congregation rose to sing 'All Things Bright and Beautiful', I remained seated and got out my phone. Holding it under cover to avoid giving offence, I searched the web for information on Arthur Drury. Miss Prim's high-pitched, determined voice rang out beside me. If she saw what I was doing, she didn't rebuke me for it.

Arthur certainly had form. It wasn't long before I found an article in a newspaper archive about an incident many years before.

Two inmates launched a violent and pre-planned attack on a prison officer at Belmarsh Prison. Brian Loughty and Arthur Drury cornered the officer in their cell and showered him with kicks and punches, knocking him unconscious.

According to the report, the prison officer had gone to check why Loughty had failed to collect his lunch from the canteen. Drury had slipped into the cell behind him, slammed the door shut and attacked him from behind. Loughty had concentrated on putting the boot in from the front.

The court heard that Drury had a lengthy history of offending, including convictions for false accounting and robbery.

Charles Ashley, defending Drury, said that his

client did not remember the incident and was sorry that the officer was hurt. Magistrates added six months to the sentences of both inmates and ordered Drury for psychiatric assessment.

I lifted my eyes from my phone to realise that the service had come to an end. The congregation were on their feet, waiting for Ma to lead them out of the chapel. She performed this duty with Jason at her side and his jailers close by. Miss Prim and I followed last, leaving Arthur in the chapel to commence the final stage of his journey alone.

Outside, the air was chilly, but it didn't dampen the enthusiasm of Jason's admirers. Once again he was surrounded, applauded and showered with words of encouragement. The police and prison officers were hard put to keep the crowd in order. But Jason's taste of freedom was brief. He was allowed one last embrace with his mother before the cuffs went back on and he disappeared into the rear of the prison van. The door banged shut, the engine started and Ma broke down completely.

'I don't want to listen to that,' Miss Prim said, so we turned our backs on Ma and went to look at the floral tributes. The tenants' wreath, organised by Miss Prim, was a dartboard of white carnations with the bullseye picked out in red. Although far from tasteful, it did at least seem appropriate – Arthur had been a dab hand at the arrows. Jason's wreath, which said *DAD* in purple flowers on a background of holly, was ghastly.

While Miss Prim was bending down to read the messages, I noticed Len Mackle, spruce in a three-piece suit and what looked like a regimental tie.

'Let's go and say hello to Len,' I said to Miss Prim.

She peered at him cautiously, then shook her head. 'I'm going to be late for my art class,' she said, and set off for the bus stop.

Len had his eyes on the row of limousines outside the chapel when I joined him. 'You were asking about Mr Vilday,' he said. 'Don't look now, but he's the one standing next to Mrs Drury.'

Vilday? At Arthur's funeral? Of course I looked. Ma was surrounded by a knot of mourners doing their best to comfort her. A tall woman was dabbing her cheeks with a tissue. A man in a black leather jacket had his arm round her shoulders.

'The one in the leather?' I said.

'That's him. The flashy one.'

'Flashy' summed him up perfectly. Greg Vilday had puffy cheeks, a snub nose and dark hair combed into an enormous quiff. The jewellery Brayne-Thompson had mentioned was out for the occasion – silver chains, bracelets, even a medallion. The overriding impression was one of massive strength. Pent-up psychopathic violence, if Brayne-Thompson was to be believed. Vilday's shoulders were almost as broad as he was tall, and his hands were like mallet heads. I remembered his middle-of-the-night phone calls. *I'd had all I could stand from Hamilton. Nobody treats me like that.* But any misgivings I felt about getting so close to him were banished by the satisfaction of having my quarry in my sights.

'You never told me Vilday knew the Drurys,' I said to Len.

He shrugged. 'In the old days, the East End crime families knew each other. They were one big unhappy family.' He sounded glad that the old days were over. 'But I must be going,' he said, looking at the stream of mourners arriving for the next cremation. 'Billy'll be wanting his break.'

We set off walking to the car park. Halfway there, Ma's limousine swept past us. I was surprised to see Greg Vilday sitting next to her on the back seat.

'Vilday and the Drurys must have been close,' I said.

'Arthur did Vilday a favour when he was a kid,' Len explained. 'Vilday has always seen him as the father he never had.' I tried to imagine a much younger Greg Vilday watching Arthur assemble his safe-cracking tools before departing on a job. And helping him unload the goods when he returned.

We arrived at the car park. Before we went our separate ways, Len stood next to his car jingling his keys as if he had something on his mind.

'If you want more background on Greg Vilday,' he said, 'I know someone who might help. A good pal of mine. Get out your phone.' He got his own out and dropped me a contact.

'Just mention Len Mackle of the Scots Guards.'

'Thanks, Len,' I said, and looked at the name he'd given me. Detective Sergeant Colin Christie (retd).

12

Colin Christie lived on an estate of modern bungalows not far from Braintree. I drove there that evening and parked in his drive behind an ageing Renault. The front lawn needed mowing and the rose bushes hadn't been pruned for years, but compared to Johnson Terrace it was decidedly middle class.

The two-tone chime brought a heavily built woman to the door, Colin's wife. I'd phoned ahead, so she was expecting me. I followed her along the hallway until we reached Colin's bedroom.

'Don't tire him,' she said in a joyless voice. 'He isn't well.'

Colin lay in a hospital-style bed in the middle of the room, surrounded by an intimidating display of medical equipment. I would have thought him too ill to receive visitors, judging by the state he was in. But as soon as I appeared in the doorway he reached eagerly for a leather strap over the bed.

'Come in, come in,' he said, pulling himself into a semi-sitting position to welcome me.

'Thanks for seeing me,' I said. I'd been expecting someone in his forties or early fifties. The man on the bed looked more like an eighty-year-old.

'I took the liberty of phoning Len after you got in touch,' Colin wheezed, letting go of the strap and sinking back into his pillow. 'He said nice things about you. What's good for Len is good enough for me, so how can I help?'

I told him I wanted to prove that Conrad Connor was innocent of the Doug Hamilton murder. As briefly as I could, I ran through the weaknesses I'd found in the prosecution case. I left Janet out of it, although I did tell him about Brayne-Thompson's phone conversations with Greg Vilday. When I said that I wanted to nail Vilday for the murder, Colin nodded.

'I wouldn't put it past him.'

'You know Vilday, then?'

Colin reached for a plastic mask on the bedside table. It was attached by tubes to a grey metallic box that made a low humming noise. He held the mask over his face for a few seconds, then told me he'd been on the team that investigated the rape allegation against Vilday. It had been his last case.

'You mean the one that collapsed?' I said. 'Len mentioned it to me. But all he knew was that Vilday had got off.'

'We were certain that Vilday was guilty,' Colin said. 'He had a record like the Black Death. What was worse, his victim was young. She made a brave effort to tell us her story, poor girl. I don't know how she managed it. She must have been beside herself, having to relive such a traumatic experience, but she gave us all we needed. Every question we put to her she answered convincingly.'

Colin paused to breathe more oxygen. I looked round at the bags of soiled linen, the medicine packs and the other sickroom odds and ends. There was a solitary rose in a vase on the mantelpiece. I thought it added a life-affirming touch, until I realised it was artificial.

Vilday's victim had visited a nightclub with a girlfriend, Colin told me when he got his breath back. She hadn't returned home by noon the next day, so her family alerted the police. They didn't mount a search immediately, advising the family that their missing daughter would probably make her own way home. But that afternoon strangers found her wandering along the Thames embankment in a state of disorientation. Concerned, they called an ambulance. It rushed her to St Thomas' Hospital, where she told staff she remembered dancing with a man in a nightclub. Later, she said, he drove her to a quiet backstreet in his car and assaulted her. The hospital alerted the police and she identified Vilday from his criminal records. The girlfriend had nothing much to add, having been separated from the victim early in the evening. But the evidence was strong enough as it stood. Tests found that the young woman had been given a date-rape drug which had interacted with the alcohol she had taken.

'We thought we had him,' Colin said. 'And that's what should have happened. But the victim withdrew her testimony. Poor kid, she was only eighteen.' He broke off, not far from tears.

I waited for him to continue.

'Anything I can do to get that bastard put away, you only have to ask,' he said with a vehemence that surprised me.

'Why did she withdraw her testimony?' I said.

'She was threatened.'

'By Vilday?'

'Who else? He's pure evil. You only have to look at him the wrong way and you get a razor across your face. No one gives evidence against Vilday.'

'Maybe that's why he was never fingered for the Doug Hamilton murder,' I said.

Colin's eyes narrowed. 'If Vilday did the Hamilton job, that would make him a double murderer. A double murderer who got away with both his crimes.'

A double murderer? I was going to ask Colin what he meant but he was overcome by a fit of coughing. He pointed a shaking finger at a bottle on the bedside table. I handed it to him and looked for a spoon. It wasn't needed. Colin drank the medicine straight from the bottle.

'Have I got this right?' I said when he'd settled down. 'Vilday has killed twice? If Doug Hamilton was one of his victims, who was the other?'

'Didn't Len tell you what happened to the woman Vilday raped?' Colin said.

The door opened and Mrs Christie swept into the room looking daggers at me.

'Is everything all right?' she asked her husband. She must have heard the coughing. 'Perhaps you need another pillow, dear.' She fetched one from a corner of the bedroom, placed it behind him and eased him into a more comfortable position.

'Not too long,' she snapped at me, then swept out again.

'You were telling me what happened to the woman Vilday raped,' I said.

'She threw herself under a train,' said Colin. 'Half an hour after she heard that the case against Vilday had been dismissed.'

Christ, I thought.

The grey metal machine beside the bed continued its monotonous humming.

'At Clapham North station. On the Northern Line.'

The enormity of Vilday's crime had silenced me. Colin stared at the ceiling, his wasted lungs fighting their losing battle. I could understand why he was bitter. If the rape had been his last case, failing to bring Vilday to justice must have been more than disappointing. As a way of rounding off a career, it was nothing short of humiliation.

'What was the young woman's name?' I said.

Colin turned his sad eyes towards me. 'Now that's something I can't tell you. She was granted anonymity, of course. Even though she's no longer with us, I think I owe it to her family to respect that.'

'It doesn't matter,' I said. 'At least I know what sort of an animal I'm after.'

'Animal is the right word.'

'I hope I didn't stay too long,' I said to Mrs Christie on my way out. 'There's a lot more I want to ask. But perhaps it's best to leave it for another day.'

She didn't reply. If I hadn't nipped out smartish, I think she would have pushed me through the door.

I stood in Colin's drive for a long time, stunned by what I had heard. Vilday's victims were coming out of the closet one by one, each demanding justice. Now there was the death of an eighteen-year-old woman against his name. I couldn't stop myself wondering whether the lawyers who got Vilday off realised that their efforts would end in tragedy at Clapham North.

13

As I'd pointed out to Len, no one had connected Conrad with the murder weapon. That placed yet another question mark against his conviction. I kicked myself for not asking Colin about Vilday's use of weapons when I had the chance, but there was no doubt that the gun had been his. *That was my gun*, he'd said to Brayne-Thompson. All I needed now was a way of proving it.

As soon as I got back to Johnson Terrace that evening, I sat down and tried to figure one out. Doug Hamilton had been killed by a 1915 Smith & Wesson revolver. It was not very different in appearance to the plastic six-shooter I'd played with as a kid. The prosecution's gun expert, a young man in a fawn suit and a snazzy waistcoat, told us they were issued to troops in large quantities during the First World War. After the armistice, they became a favourite with criminals across Europe. This was because they were widely available and the ammunition was easy to come by. Fast forward a century, and many of them were still in circulation. To make matters worse, some foreign countries no longer classified them as firearms because of their age. They were regarded as antiques, and that meant they could be traded legally. Getting hold of one was a doddle, the expert said, if you knew where to go.

My thoughts were interrupted by a loud knocking on the front door. This was unusual because Flats 1 and 2 had their own bells. The knocking continued a long time. I was about to go down when George beat me to it. The sound of him opening the front door was followed by a low buzz of conversation.

'Tony!' he shouted up the stairs. 'It's for you.'

As I went down I caught a glimpse of George vanishing into his flat. He'd left the front door wide open. The caller, visible in the light from the hall, was well into his sixties if not older.

'Mr Quirke?' he enquired when I went up to him.

'That's me,' I said, wondering if he'd ever been a boxer. He was completely bald, his nose had been broken at some point and he had scars on his chin. I was about to ask him what he wanted when a figure stepped out from behind him, a taller man in a pork pie hat and dark glasses.

'Can we have a word?' the one in the dark glasses said.

'What about?'

The bald man's body tensed. Looking down, I saw that he'd clenched his fist as if he was going to throw a punch at me. Although he wasn't young, he looked fit. I tried to shut the door in his face but wasn't quick enough. He pushed his way in like a tank going through a privet hedge.

'Can we come in?' the one in the dark glasses said, stepping into the hall behind his companion.

'No,' I said. 'I'd rather you left.'

They didn't like me saying that. The bald one gave me some vicious shoves in the chest. I came straight back at him and tried to hustle him towards the door. All it earned me was a punch in the solar plexus. Only a boxer could have thrown a punch like that, I remember thinking as I doubled up gasping for breath.

'Look here—' I began, but it was difficult to get the words out.

More shoves forced me against the wall. Hands on my shoulders pinned me there. The bald man's face was only a couple of inches away from mine. He had clear blue eyes, I noticed.

'We don't like what you're up to,' he said.

His breath forced me to turn my head to one side.

'We want you to stop,' he said.

'Stop what?'

He looked round at his companion without taking any pressure off my shoulders. 'Did you hear that? Stop what, he says.'

The man in the dark glasses laughed.

'Stop poking your nose into other people's business, that's what. This is a polite request to call it off. Why don't you? It's in your own interest.'

I was still keeping my head to one side.

'We think you ought to fuck off back where you come from,' the man in the dark glasses added.

'George!' I shouted. We were only a few feet from his door.

'Shut your mouth,' the bald one said.

'That's not very nice,' I replied.

The bald one looked at his companion again. 'Funny man,' he said. 'What do I do with him now?'

'I think he wants you to hit him,' came the reply.

Halitosis notwithstanding, I turned my head and looked straight into my tormentor's eyes. 'Fuck you,' I said and kneed him where he was least expecting it. It wasn't enough to floor him, but it was enough to take the pressure off my shoulders. Slipping out of his grasp, I ran for the stairs and took them two at a time. Hands grabbed the back of my shirt before I'd got halfway up, but I managed to kick out behind me. My heel connected with something soft.

Looking round, I saw the one in the dark glasses clutching his face as he fell backwards, his hat spinning over the banisters. The bald one was having difficulty getting past him. It gave me enough time to reach my flat and lock the door.

It didn't give me enough time to reach my phone. I'd left it in my jacket on the back of my chair. I started across the room to retrieve it, but a couple of seconds later there was a terrific thump on the door and it bowed inwards. I didn't have a deadlock or a bolt like George. All I had was a rim lock held on by four small screws.

There was no way it would stand up to treatment like that. I had to forget the phone and put my shoulder against the door.

'Whose business am I supposed to be poking into?' I shouted.

There was no reply. The door sprang back into shape, but I didn't dare take my shoulder away. I could hear voices on the other side. I couldn't make out what they were saying, but they didn't sound friendly.

'I think you ought to go,' I yelled.

There was more mumbling on the other side of the door. I looked at my jacket and wondered how long it would take to get across the room, retrieve my phone and call for help. Too long, I decided.

'George!' I shouted.

'Come on, mate, let us in,' one of them said in a wheedling tone. Judging by the Estuary accent, it was the one in the dark glasses. The bald one sounded more south of the river.

'George!'

'We only want to chat,' the wheedling continued.

Of course they did. 'You can talk to me like this,' I shouted.

The suggestion was met with silence. Seconds later, I heard feet clumping down the stairs and the sound of the front door opening. But only one pair of feet had gone down and I could hear breathing on the other side of the door. I kept my shoulder where it was.

The next attempt came without warning. Wood cracked as the door bent inwards. Once again I managed to hold it. What I needed was something to wedge it shut so that I could get to my phone. The cheap pine bed was too light. The wardrobe would have been ideal, but I couldn't heave it into position without leaving the door undefended. What else was there?

Sliding one foot backwards, I managed to hook it round the nearest table leg. Without taking my shoulder away from the door, I tried to drag the table towards me. The sound of scraping across bare boards was answered by yet another shove on the door. I had to unhook my foot so that I could push back hard enough.

The next heave nearly took the door off its hinges. Once again I forced it back. Once again my opponent tried to force it open. We see-sawed like this for a couple of minutes, then the door went straight. The rim lock was doing better than I'd expected, but I was worried about the hinges.

'My neighbour's calling the police,' I yelled.

The door bowed inwards again. Wall plaster fell at my feet.

'George!' I shouted. What was he doing? Hiding behind one of his faux-leather easy chairs?

Hooking my foot round the table leg again, I managed to shift it a few extra inches. But it jammed against a warped floorboard.

Shit.

There was a short period of inactivity, then I heard the front door slam and feet came pounding up the stairs. The other one had returned. God knows what he'd brought with him, but it was heavy. He aimed the first blow immediately behind the lock. More plaster fell out of the wall.

'Maniacs,' I shouted.

Another thump followed, accompanied by the worst splintering yet. There was nothing I could do. The door gave way and they were in.

Squaring up to me, the bald one punched me so hard in the chest that I fell over. Then he put the boot in. The first kick went into my side. My body responded by tightening itself into a ball. The next kick opened me out again.

'I could have killed you,' he said. The words came faintly, as if they'd been spoken in another room. 'Give us any more trouble and I will.'

The other one started to stamp on my legs. 'Fucking get out of here,' he screamed. 'Fuck off home! Now!'

There was a moment of blackness. Then there was someone bending over me. He wore dark glasses and there were streaks of blood on his face. He didn't say anything. When he disappeared from view, I thought he'd decided that I'd had enough. But he was positioning himself for a running kick. This time I actually saw the pain. It wrapped itself round me like a sheet of orange flame.

14

A couple of days later I was let into Janet's flat by a man in a grey T-shirt. He was about the same age as me, thick-set and muscular with a high-and-tight haircut. He didn't say a word when I told him I'd come to see Janet. After looking curiously at the sticking plaster on the bridge of my nose, he turned on his heel and led me into the living room.

Janet was lounging on the sofa, dressed in jeans and a white sweater.

'Is it all right to talk?' I said, indicating her companion. She hadn't mentioned anybody else when I'd phoned to arrange our meeting.

'You mean Rick?' she replied. 'Rick is OK. He knows everything. There isn't a problem with Rick.'

'Hello, Tony.' Rick didn't offer me his hand and didn't smile as he greeted me.

'Come and sit down,' Janet said. She swung her legs off the sofa and I sat beside her. There wasn't anywhere else. Rick took up a position on the other side of the room and his eyes never left me. I got the impression he didn't trust me alone with her.

Janet leaned forward, studied my face and frowned. 'What have you been up to, Tony?'

I told her how Vilday's bully boys had given me a going over. My downstairs neighbour had emerged from his flat after they'd gone, I said, and called an ambulance. I'd spent the night in A&E. But I wasn't giving up.

Janet was horrified. 'Oh my God,' she said, 'I never thought anything like this would happen. Now you know why Mr Brayne-Thompson didn't want to go to the police.'

I couldn't say I hadn't been warned.

'Are you feeling OK?'

'I'll get over it,' I said.

She looked relieved. But I hadn't come in search of sympathy. I wanted to update her on where things stood. I told her about spotting Vilday at Arthur's funeral, then about my visit to Colin Christie. Janet heard me out without saying a word.

On my walk from Kilburn station to her flat, I'd been trying to figure out how to link Vilday to the murder weapon. 'According to Colin,' I said, 'Vilday's a slippery character. We're going to need solid evidence to use against him. And the man to get it from is Brayne-Thompson. He's the only person who knows him inside out. We'll have to meet with him again. There must be a lot more he could tell us about his favourite client.'

I was surprised to see Janet shaking her head. 'I've discussed all that with Rick,' she said. 'We don't think it would be a good idea.'

I tried to explain what I meant. 'We need info on Vilday that'll link him to the crime, and that's the angle Brayne-Thompson's got on him. That's all I'm saying.'

'Surely you don't want him to get away with it?'

'Of course I don't,' I said. 'But when Brayne-Thompson next sees Vilday, he can ask him what sort of gun he was talking about in those midnight conversations. Doug Hamilton was killed with a Smith & Wesson revolver. That's the crucial link between the murder and the murderer. If we could find evidence—'

'But we promised Mr Brayne-Thompson we would never speak to him again.'

Janet didn't give me time to reply. Without another word, she got up from the sofa and joined Rick on the other side of the room. Wrapping her arms tightly around her sides, she leaned back against the wall and looked at me through suspicious eyes. I found her behaviour hard to understand. It seemed that everything I said was wrong. Whenever I suggested doing something about her brother's conviction, she found a reason for questioning it.

'Vilday,' Rick said. 'You do agree he's lower than vermin, don't you?'

I didn't answer him. Of course I knew what sort of a person Vilday was.

'Now that he's on to you,' Janet said, 'we'll have to move fast.'

I still couldn't understand why she was behaving like this.

Rick strolled forward and stood in front of me with his hands in the pockets of his jeans. 'There's only one way to deal with Greg Vilday,' he said, looking down at me.

'Kill him,' said Janet from the other side of the room.

I wasn't sure I'd heard her right. 'What on earth do you mean?' I said.

They stared at me as if I was stupid. 'Take him out,' Rick said. 'That's what we mean.'

Janet's brother had been wrongfully convicted of murder and she was talking about committing murder herself? This was beyond insane.

'I don't get it,' I said. 'I thought we were trying to put Vilday in the dock.'

'Why do you want to bring the law into it?' Janet said. 'You know they won't do anything.' I looked at her in amazement. This wasn't the Janet I knew. When she stopped me in the street after the trial, I could feel her pain. All I could see in this Janet's eyes was malice. There's a way of doing things, I wanted to tell her. We only need to get the evidence together and Vilday will go to prison. But I'd already told her that.

'I don't think we ought to be talking about murder,' I said.

'That's a pity,' Rick said, and swayed back on his heels as if I'd insulted him.

'You don't seem to be all there,' Janet said.

'That's right,' Rick added. 'We can't quite suss you out. One minute you tell us you're up for it, next minute you're pulling out. We don't know where we stand, honestly we don't.'

Janet curled her lip. 'How long do you think you'll stay alive if you shop Vilday to the filth?'

I stood up, faced Rick and spoke quietly. 'If you'll move out of my way, I'll be leaving. I've got a train to catch.'

'No you haven't,' Rick said. We stood there glaring at each other for a few seconds. Then he pulled his hands out of his pockets, grabbed my right arm and forced it up my back. It was hours since I'd taken a tablet and I yelled with pain. Who is he? I asked myself. Janet's boyfriend? Her husband? A brother I'd never heard about? They seemed close, that much was clear. Why had she never mentioned him?

Spinning me round as if we were wrestlers in a ring, Rick threw me back on the sofa. I landed hard and it hurt. I looked round for Janet but she'd disappeared. She didn't want to watch the rough stuff, I assumed, and prepared myself for more. Wriggling into a less uncomfortable position, I looked up at Rick. He was standing over me, legs apart, fists clenched, waiting for me to fight back. I wasn't minded to, not for the second time in as many days. I shielded my head with my arms. Then Janet reappeared, pulling a pair of straight-backed chairs behind her.

Mystified, I kept my arms wrapped round my head while Rick placed the chairs in front of me. Janet disappeared again. The way she and Rick worked was so sharp I wondered how long they'd been practising.

'You mug!' Rick said, taking a seat on one of the chairs, crossing his legs and looking down at me with a lopsided grin on his face.

'There's no need for this,' I said.

Rick's grin got broader.

I wondered if I could knock him off the chair. I decided I couldn't, not from my position on the sofa. 'You're making a mistake,' I said.

Rick carried on grinning.

Janet made another of her entrances. This time she was carrying a cardboard box seven or eight inches square. She sat on the chair next to Rick with the box on her knees.

'Don't you think the world would be a nicer place if we got rid of him?' Rick said.

I stopped shielding my head and concentrated on trying to ease my aching side.

'Believe me,' Rick went on, 'Vilday's done a lot of harm. No one can do what he's done and expect to get away with it. It's not right. I don't see why we should eat shit on his behalf. But no one's going to do it for us. We're going to have to fix him on our own.'

'You're getting things out of proportion,' I said.

Janet handed the cardboard box to Rick.

'You can do what you like,' I said, 'as long as you don't drag me into it.'

'Shall I tell you what you are?' Rick was holding the cardboard box as if there was something precious in it. 'You're a Frankie Howard.'

He took the lid off the box and brought out a small

object wrapped in cloth, handling it the way a priest might handle a holy relic. The shape was unmistakable. It wasn't holy and it wasn't a relic. Rick unwound the cloth and showed it to me. The colour was black, or perhaps very dark grey with a blue tinge, and the barrel was short and ugly.

'Know what this is?'

I knew exactly what it was but shook my head.

'It's for you,' Janet said. 'You're going to kill Vilday for us.'

Rick raised the gun in a slow, deliberate movement and aimed it at my head.

I stared down the barrel.

He pulled the trigger.

Click.

My heart stampeded.

'For Christ's sake, Rick,' I yelled. 'Have you gone mad?'

'What's that?' he said. 'Are you trying to say no? Are you telling us you don't think Vilday ought to pay the price?' He was enjoying himself. 'We were expecting better than this, Tony. You're a disappointment to us.'

All I could do was shake my head.

'I'll ask you one more time. How'd you like to take Vilday out for us?'

'Why don't you do it yourselves?' I said. 'Why are you asking me?'

'Ah,' said Rick, 'good question. Because they'll never trace it back to you, that's why. Not like they could trace it back to us. They'd know it was us because we've got reason to do it. You haven't. They'll never connect it to you.'

'You can't expect me to go along with this,' I said. 'It's murder. I can't do anything like that. How long do you think I'd get for murder?'

'You won't,' Janet said. 'Because you won't get caught. We've worked out exactly what you have to do. Don't worry, there's no risk. When it's over, you can forget it ever happened.'

The realisation hit me like a punch in the face. 'You've been planning this all along, haven't you? You never had any intention of appealing Conrad's conviction. All you ever wanted—'

I stopped because of the way Janet was looking at me. The face that stared down from the straight-backed chair, the face I'd seen full of despair in the street after the trial, was now merciless. Her grief must have turned her mind. The signs had been there all along. The mood swings. The secretiveness. The outbursts. If only I'd been smart enough to recognise them sooner.

'It'll be easy,' she said. Standing up, she walked round the back of the sofa, put her hands on my shoulders and started massaging my neck. Her hands were warm and I could smell her perfume. Every time she broke off to run her fingers through my hair, I cringed.

'The gun we've got you is perfect for the job,' she said. 'You can slip it in your pocket and no one will know it's there.'

Rick was fondling it affectionately, weighing it in his hand, stroking the grip with his stubby fingers. 'It's

Austrian,' he said. 'Why can't we make beautiful things like this in England?'

It was the ugliest thing I'd seen in my life.

'Tomorrow lunchtime,' Janet said, 'Vilday will be drinking in his favourite pub. It's where he always goes. Rick will drive you there. You'll go in, walk up to him, do the business and drop the gun on the floor. No one will try to stop you. They'll be shitting themselves. You'll walk out nice and calm and Rick will bring you back here. After that, you can disappear and we'll never bother you again.'

'This is crazy.'

'Was that another no?' Janet stopped working my neck.

'Sure as hell it was,' Rick said.

Janet sighed. 'If you're not going to help us, there's no way we can help you. Be sensible. Trust us. Do what we say and you'll be safe as houses.'

'This is an awful thing you're asking me to do, Janet.'

'What happens now, Rick?' she said.

Rick's answer was to drag me off the sofa, force me to the floor and sit on me. Once more I howled with pain. He held my wrists behind my back while Janet tied them together. Then he dragged me to my feet and sat me on one of the straight-backed chairs.

'It looks like the little piggies,' he said.

'Oh dear,' said Janet. 'I don't like going to Ongar. Do we have to?'

'He's forcing our hand.'

'Shall I get the plastic sheets?'

140

'Just a minute, I'll ask him one more time. What's it to be, Tony?'

'I don't know what's got into you,' I said. 'This is madness—' My voice failed when I saw the knife in Rick's hand.

'Now,' he said, 'are you right-handed or left-handed?'

'I think he's right-handed,' Janet said.

Rick bent me forward, reached behind my back and took hold of my right hand. 'I'll start with the pinkie.'

My scalp tightened.

'It's your own fault,' he said. 'We were hoping you'd see a bit of sense.'

The blade touched my little finger behind the knuckle.

'I've got a better idea,' Janet said. 'Get his pants down.'

Rick let go of my hand, pulled me off the chair and hurled me on the sofa again. Then he was kneeling on top of me, fumbling with my belt, unzipping my flies and dragging my jeans down to my knees. Over his shoulder I could see Janet laughing at me. She was holding the knife with the blade against her cheek.

'Know what?' she said. 'I think he's going to change his mind.'

'I'll do it!' I screamed. 'I'll kill Vilday for you. But for Christ's sake, put that fucking knife away!'

15

It was beginning to get light when I heard a key in the lock. The bedroom they'd put me in overnight was not much bigger than the double bed it contained. The only other item of furniture was a full-length swing mirror. I'd spent a sleepless night staring at myself staring at myself in this mirror. My mouth tasted sour, the air was stale with sweat and they'd taken my phone away.

'Wakey-wakey,' said Rick from the doorway. He was carrying a brown leather holdall. 'Ever use a shooter?'

I shook my head.

'Didn't think so.'

I had to assume he had the gun on him. And that it was loaded. 'A cup of tea would be nice,' I said.

I followed him into the kitchen. He dropped the holdall on the floor and flicked the switch of an electric kettle. Reaching inside a supermarket bag on the worktop, he pulled out a jar of coffee, two plastic mugs, a carton of milk and a bag of sugar. He searched the kitchen drawers for cutlery but they were empty, so he took the lid off the jar, shook granules into the mugs and made us coffee. In the absence of a spoon to stir it with, he produced a ballpoint pen from his back pocket. Self-sufficient hardly described him. I wondered if he'd ever served in the military.

Next out of the bag came a couple of buns. I tore the cellophane off mine like a starving beggar. Cheese and bacon. My stomach almost leapt out of my throat to get at it. After we'd finished, Rick crumpled the wrappings and looked round for a bin. There wasn't one, so he dropped them on the floor.

'The pub's called the Tied Struggler,' he said.

'Christ's sake, Rick, there'll be dozens of witnesses. Why don't we go to Vilday's home? Do him on his doorstep when there's no one about? I know where he lives.'

Rick shook his head. 'Vilday's house is like Fort Knox. Anyone can walk into the Struggler. And what's more important, walk out again.'

'What about CCTV?'

'No one will recognise you. You'll be wearing a mask. But we'll discuss that when you've learned to shoot.'

'I'm not sure I like this,' I said.

'You'll find your man at the bar on the ground floor,' Rick said. He produced a sheaf of photos, shots of the Tied Struggler inside and out. You couldn't mistake its black-and-white Tudor-style frontage, with the hanging baskets trailing flowers down to the pavement. The layout inside was a typical roadhouse pub, deep leather sofas in the window alcoves and plenty of space to walk about in. The bar had a row of glass display cabinets to one side of the beer taps. That's where Vilday would be drinking, perched on a bar stool, Rick told me. He pointed to the interior columns with shelves for customers to rest their glasses on. There'd be drinkers standing round them, he said, and they could block my getaway. So when I was heading for the exit I should do a dog leg. By that he meant walk from the bar to the corner where the gents was, then continue along the wood-panelled wall to the swing doors. He'd be waiting for me in his car outside with the engine running, he said. Walk nice and calm, don't run. And keep your mask on until you're in the car.

After we'd looked through the shots of the Struggler, Rick showed me another bundle of photos. They were all of Vilday.

'But you've seen him, you said?'

'That's right.' I didn't need to look twice at the podgy face and voluminous quiff, the black leather jacket and the silver chains, bracelets and medallions.

'Time to go to school,' said Rick. 'How to use the PK-32.'

'The what?'

'The little beauty I showed you yesterday. The Kofler PK-32. Remember?'

Out of his holdall came an object wrapped in black plastic. He placed it on the worktop. 'I spent a long time last night cleaning it with bleach,' he said. 'From now on you don't touch it, see?'

'How can I shoot Vilday if I don't touch it?'

'Wear a pair of these.' Two packets of latex gloves joined the gun on the worktop. Rick suddenly looked serious. 'So how do you feel about what we're going to do today? Go on, tell me.'

'I don't have a problem with it,' I said. 'Vilday's long overdue.'

My reply seemed to please him. 'You're facing up to it very well,' he said. 'It's difficult the first time you top someone. But don't think you haven't got the capacity. Everyone has. It's just a matter of bringing it out in you.'

The front door of the flat opened with a crash then slammed shut. Someone marched through the living room and into the kitchen. It was Janet, pulling a carry-on case. She looked tense. But when she saw me her face broke into a smile.

'You've made the right decision,' she said, throwing her arms around my neck and kissing me full on the mouth. 'The little piggies will have to go without their dinner.'

Rick's car was a grey Vauxhall that badly needed a wash – the sort you see every day and don't pay much attention to. From the way he drove, I got the impression it didn't belong to him.

'Where are you taking me?' I said.

'Epping Forest.'

It was a long drive, and neither of us spoke on the way. When we arrived, Rick turned into a car park. It was deserted, as you would expect on a weekday in the middle of September.

'That's where we're going,' he said, pointing to some distant trees. We got out of the car and started to tramp across the wet grass, a bitter north-easterly blowing in our faces. When we reached the trees, Rick kept walking and didn't slow down. We went deep into the forest. The paths between the trees were muddy, so he decided to go off-piste, striking a new route across mounds of fallen leaves. It would have made a pleasant autumn walk if I'd known where we were going, or what was going to happen when we got there. We kept it up for what felt like miles before Rick stopped at the edge of a large hollow. 'This is it,' he said.

The hollow was about ten feet deep, overgrown with bushes and stunted trees. We clambered down its steep side and fought our way through the undergrowth. Rick seemed to know exactly where he was going. After a while we came to a little clearing. It was even muddier than the paths through the forest, and there was a lot of rubbish scattered about. But it was secluded. I guess that was what Rick wanted.

He pulled the packets of latex gloves out of his holdall and we put them on. Then, very carefully, he took the PK-32 out of its plastic bag and handed it to me. It was the first time I'd held a gun. The thought of what I was supposed to do with it produced a sudden urge to throw it away. But it fitted into my hand so neatly that it soon felt part of me. That was the surprising thing. It wasn't as heavy as I'd expected – after I'd waved it around a few times, I hardly knew it was there.

'It's a semi-automatic,' Rick said.

'Is it,' I said, not knowing what that meant.

Rick indicated a tree. 'Aim at that beech. Imagine it's Greg Vilday. Then pull the trigger.'

The beech tree was about five yards away. I pointed the gun and thought of Doug Hamilton lying in a pool of his own blood. But when it came to pulling the trigger, my finger wouldn't obey me. So I thought of the eighteen-year-old Vilday had raped and driven to suicide. It was the only way I could do what Rick wanted.

I pulled the trigger.

Nothing happened.

'You're going to like using a shooter,' Rick said. 'I can tell.' Taking it back, he showed me how to load it. The procedure was simplicity itself. He pulled the magazine out of the bottom of the grip, filled it with seven live cartridges and snapped it back in. Holding the gun with both hands, he fired at the tree. A piece of bark flew off, leaving an ugly white patch. Another surprising thing – the gun didn't make much noise. It was more of a whack than a bang, but it was accompanied by an awful lot of smoke.

'Now it's your turn,' he said. 'I'll talk you through it.'

I listened to Rick's instructions in a daze. I'd disagreed with the other members of a jury, so now I was to become a public executioner? But I did everything he told me. I held the PK-32 with both hands, the way you're supposed to. I fired off scores of rounds. The barrel became hot to the touch, and a lot of bark was blasted off a lot of trees.

When Rick thought I'd made enough progress, we climbed out of the hollow and walked back to the car park. We could have been a couple of gunslingers in a Western, me with the fully-loaded PK-32 in the pocket of my jeans.

It was now mine.

'How d'you feel?' Rick said with one of his funny smiles as we came out of the woods and saw his car in the distance.

'What do you mean?'

'Having a gun on you,' he said. 'Makes you feel good, does it?' He leaned over and slapped the pocket where I'd put the PK-32. 'Makes you feel ten feet tall?'

'Twenty feet,' I said, watching him out of the corner of my eye.

'It makes me feel fucking wonderful,' he said, swaggering like a kid in a playground.

'Oh,' I said. 'You've got a gun too, have you?'

He laughed. 'You don't think I'd let you loose with the PK-32 without having a shooter of my own, do you?'

No, I hadn't thought that for a moment. It was why I hadn't made a run for it.

'Yeah,' he said, swaggering some more. 'Fucking ten feet tall.'

We got back into the car, drove out of the forest and found a café where we had a bite to eat. When we'd finished, Rick pulled out a bottle of pills. He shook two into his cupped hand and offered them to me.

I hesitated.

'Go on,' he said. 'They're harmless. Musicians gobble them all the time. They stop you feeling nervous.'

'What are they?'

'They're all right,' he said. 'Look, I'll show you.' He swallowed the pills with a mouthful of coffee. Then he shook two more out of the bottle for me.

16

We drove southwards. 'Hang on,' I reminded Rick. 'You said I could have my phone back.'

He gave me a dirty look. 'When you've taken Vilday out. When I pick you up afterwards.'

'I want it now. Suppose something goes wrong and I need to phone you?'

'Nothing will go wrong.'

'I want my phone.'

Rick's hands tightened on the steering wheel. 'Why? Who are you thinking of phoning?'

'Nobody.'

'What's the point of having a phone if you're not phoning anybody?'

'Come on, Rick.'

He looked as if he was wrestling with the biggest decision of his life. 'You're not thinking of double-crossing us, are you?' he said. 'Because if you do, the last thing you'll see will be the inside of an industrial meat mincer. We've got one, you know.'

'Bloody hell,' I said, 'I already told you. Vilday's got it coming. The bastard put me in hospital. I'm looking forward to it.'

Once again, I seemed to have satisfied him. My phone was in the glove compartment, he told me. I got it out and stuffed it in my pocket.

'By the way,' I said, 'what are these pigs you keep talking about?'

'Our uncle's got a farm full of them,' Rick said. 'Near Ongar.' He wrinkled his nose. 'Don't half fucking smell.'

We drove on in silence. I got more nervous with every mile that passed. Vilday's chubby cheeks and greasy quiff appeared in front of me like an apparition. Rick had told me to walk up to him, whip out the PK-32, press the muzzle hard against his chest and pull the trigger. It seemed so simple, but I was shaking at the thought of it. The pills didn't seem to be working.

'Christ,' Rick said, glancing at his watch. 'Better get a move on.'

He accelerated. Terraced houses flashed past, then gave way to suburban semis. The semis were followed by detached houses and within minutes we were driving past terraces again. We were travelling east on a congested A road, way above the limit, overtaking when we could. We went through Ilford, Goodmayes and Rush Green. The traffic thinned and we took a right.

'Not far now,' Rick said with another glance at his watch.

I looked in the wing mirror. We were being tailed by a patrol car.

Rick saw it at the same time. 'Fuck! Fuck! Fuck!' he shouted, accelerating wildly as he fumbled in his pocket. 'Here, take this.'

I looked at what he'd dropped in my lap. It was his gun. A big black snub-nosed shooter.

'Get rid of it,' he told me. 'Yours as well. Out the fucking window! Now!'

He was driving like a madman, throwing the Vauxhall down narrow roads lined with parked vehicles, swerving round corners, narrowly missing pedestrians. The patrol car switched on its siren and stayed on our tail. I had to admire Rick's skill behind the wheel. But he was never going to shake off the patrol car. When we reached a wider stretch of road, it shot past with its lights flashing and blocked our way.

Rick stood on the brakes. As soon as we shuddered to a halt, I threw the passenger door open and jumped out. The patrol car was backing up fast, its engine screaming. There were at least three uniformed officers inside.

I didn't waste time thinking about it. I made off in the opposite direction as fast as I could, without the faintest idea of where I was going. The road ahead was one of those North London thoroughfares that go on for ever. It was only a matter of time before they'd catch up with me. But within minutes I came to a narrow alleyway. I couldn't see the other end because it curved to the left. It could have been a dead end but I went down it, between back gardens at first, past a play park and then between the blank walls of tall buildings. Finally, I came out on a busy high street.

People were strolling past, old folk with trolleys, mothers with baby buggies, school kids munching chips. Where now? Immediately in front of me a pedestrian crossing had just changed lights. I could hear the sound of boots pounding hell for leather along the alleyway, so I followed the stream of pedestrians across the road. At the other side I faced an even bigger decision. Left or right? This was a part of London I didn't know. I looked for an Underground sign but couldn't see one. To my right, a long queue was waiting at a bus stop. I thought of joining it but there wasn't a bus in sight. To my left, the street was teeming with shoppers. All I could hope for was to lose myself in the crowd, so I turned left.

Walking as briskly as I could, fighting the impulse to look behind me, I began to think that I was going to get away with it. But I had to step aside to avoid colliding with an impatient-looking businessman. My way was then blocked by racks of fruit and vegetables sticking out in front of a shop. It was a white-knuckle moment, but it saved me. If I'd continued along the high street, what every instinct in my body was telling me to do, I wouldn't have noticed the shop. It called itself an International Food and Wine Supermarket. I made straight for the entrance.

Once through the dangling strips of blue and white plastic, I grabbed a wire basket and strolled along the aisles.

I was doing my best to look like a customer. Outwardly, I might have appeared interested in the products on the shelves. Inwardly, I was a tightly wound spring, waiting for the police to come charging in.

Forcing myself to take a carton of coconut milk off a shelf, I turned it over in my hand and looked at the sell-by date. My mind registered nothing. I put it back and studied the intertwining B and S on a tin of Keralan coconut curry. I had never taken so much interest in trademarks. Did the delicate fronds represent spices? There was no way of telling.

Before submitting a jar of mango chutney to similar scrutiny, I risked a quick peek at the entrance. The plastic strips parted and my heart missed a beat. But the incomer was nobody more threatening than a short, middle-aged woman. She went straight to the household goods section, I took a deep breath and my eyes went back to the shelves. Coriander naan bread. Next to it, plain naan bread. I rather prefer the coriander, I said to myself, but left it where it was.

Clutching my wire basket to my side, I let the minutes tick away. Where had my pursuers got to? The silence inside the shop was unnerving. I strained my ears for noises from the street. A passing bus ground its gears, a car horn honked. Everything sounded normal. I almost burst out laughing. I'd thrown them off.

What would I have told them if they'd nabbed me? Everything? Nothing? It was chilling to realise that I had no idea. If I did admit what Rick and I were up to, would I then say that I had no intention of shooting Vilday?

That I'd only pretended to go along with Rick's insane plan until I got the opportunity to do a runner? That as soon as he dropped me outside the Tied Struggler, I was going to leg it down the road and put him and Janet behind me for ever? That was the truth. But what good had the truth done my father? The police aren't interested in the truth. They're interested in convictions.

By now an uneventful fifteen minutes had passed, so I decided it was safe to break cover. But my wire basket was empty. I didn't want to walk out without buying anything – the lad on the checkout might think that I'd been stealing. He might call the police. How ironic would that be? I picked up a can of fizzy drink and a cellophane-wrapped steak pie and made my way to the checkout.

'I'll take these,' I said, unloading my purchases. 'And can you tell me if there's a Tube or railway station near here?'

'District Line, sir,' the lad said. 'It's immediately behind us, but you can't get there direct. You'll have to turn right out of the shop and follow the road down to the bottom. Turn right at the bottom, then right again and you'll see the station ahead of you.'

That would suit me fine. I thanked him, walked out of the supermarket with my lunch and found myself face to face with a policeman.

17

He'd spotted me the moment I pushed through the plastic strips. Something about me had made him suspicious. It could have been the way I reacted when our eyes met. I'd taken an instinctive step backwards, and that's not what innocent citizens do. It's what thieves do. Or fugitives.

He could have been one of the coppers who'd chased me down the alley. Or he could have been another one. Whoever he was, he gave me a 'What have we got here?' look and decided that he needed to find out.

I ducked inside the shop again. That only made matters worse, because I bumped into the middle-aged shopper on her way out. 'Ooft,' she protested and dropped the bag she was carrying. We stood there glaring at each other as loose apples rolled on the floor between us.

'Do you mind?' she said.

Without thinking, I whipped out the Batman mask Rick had given me and put it on. It made the woman back away. But the entrance was narrow, so I had to give her a shove to get past.

'Get off me! Get off!'

'Is there a problem?' I heard the policeman ask the lad on the checkout as I hurried to the rear of the shop.

'He's over there!' the woman shouted from the entrance, pointing in my direction. 'He assaulted me.'

'Excuse me, sir—'

It was only a mini supermarket, twenty or thirty paces from the checkout to where I was standing. Realising that I had to move fast, I looked for a rear exit. The eyeholes in the mask didn't give much of a view, but they were enough to reveal a shop assistant standing in an open doorway. She must have been wondering what the noise was about. Whatever she'd been expecting, it couldn't have been Batman.

'Just a minute, sir—'

The officer was halfway down the aisle.

I went up to the shop assistant. 'Let me through.'

She didn't move, so I grabbed her by the shoulders and pushed her backwards. Not roughly, but firmly. She screamed and dropped the broom she'd been carrying.

Looking around me, I realised that although I was through the doorway, it wasn't the rear exit I'd taken it to be. I was in a storeroom. Within its narrow confines, the shop assistant's screams sounded louder than they probably were. Lifting a corner of the mask, I saw a female of about sixteen or seventeen pressing herself against the far wall. Her face was bright red from the noise she was making. But it was her eyes that struck me most. They were as wide as dinner plates and fixed on me in terror. It wasn't the effect I'd intended to have, but there was no time to apologise.

Remembering the policeman, I turned my back on her and slammed the storeroom door. Then I examined the catch. Good, it had a deadbolt. I snapped it on – just in time, because seconds later someone tried the handle from outside. When the door wouldn't budge, they started thumping it with what sounded like their fists.

'Open up! Police!'

A deadbolt can be unlocked from the outside. The lad on the checkout was probably fetching the key. I went back to the shop assistant.

'Is there another way out of here?'

She slid down the wall until she was sitting on the floor, pulled her knees up to her chest and the screaming got worse.

'Open up! Police!'

The storeroom walls were lined with shelves packed with plastic crates. There was also a flatbed trolley loaded with wire shopping baskets, a bike propped against a wall, cleaning equipment and some empty display stands. But not the slightest indication of another way out. It was a dead end. The prospect of being served up on a platter for another Jolliffe was not an attractive one.

The shop assistant's screams were getting more frantic than ever. Panic grabbed me by the throat. Without a conscious decision, I threw the shopping baskets off the trolley and started replacing them with crates from the shelves. I chose crates that were full to the brim with produce – shrink-wrapped six-packs of fizzy drinks, condiment bottles, bagged-up vegetables, washing liquid, soap. The heavier the better. Then I pushed the fully loaded trolley towards the door and began stacking the crates against it. By the time I'd finished, sweat was running down my face inside the mask and soaking my shirt.

But there wouldn't be enough of them to hold the door. Lifting a corner of the mask again, my eyes fell on the empty display stands. Dragging one over, I jammed the top under the door handle, then took another stand and laid it flat on the ground to hold the first one in position. A couple of sturdy plastic crates filled the gap between the second display stand and the wall. I was getting good at this.

Thump. For a stunned moment I wondered what had hit me on the head. *Thump.* It hit me again. Turning round, I realised that the screaming had stopped. The shop assistant was standing in front of me, bent at the knees as if she was facing-off in a hockey match. Instead of a hockey stick, she was holding a long-handled mop. The mop was only plastic, but it hurt when she jabbed me in the face and nearly knocked my mask off. I took three or four steps back.

'I'm not going to harm you,' I said, raising my hands in a gesture of submission.

She bared her teeth and gave me another jab with the mop. Feeling that the room was closing in on me, I retreated even further. It was only then that I noticed the glass door. It was a fire exit. There had to be one. The display stands had been leaning against it, which was why I hadn't seen it before. But I'd backed off so far that the shop assistant was blocking my way.

'I'm only passing through,' I said.

Her answer was another jab in the face.

'There isn't any need for this,' I said. 'Just step aside and I'll be gone in a tick.'

She tensed herself for her next move, a mad rush at me if her previous behaviour was anything to go by. I moved back even further.

Then we both heard it. Someone inserting a key in the lock. And turning it, and opening the door until it jammed on the display stand.

'Police! Get back against the wall. Police!'

'He's in here!' the shop assistant shouted.

A succession of violent shoves on the door buckled the top of the display stand. There was nothing else I could do. Reaching into my pocket, I brought out the Kofler PK-32. The shop assistant's eyes fastened on it and the mop fell to the floor. Slowly, I raised it the way Rick had raised it on me and aimed it at her head. Her flushed cheeks went white.

'Move back.'

She moved back a couple of paces, her eyes never leaving the gun.

'Back to the far end.'

She shuffled back until she reached the wall.

'Turn round.'

She stayed as she was.

'I said turn round and face the wall.'

She was looking at the door. By now the display stand had almost been knocked away. The gap in the door had opened enough to let a policeman's arm through. It was feeling round for the obstruction.

'Don't move an inch,' I said to the shop assistant, crammed the PK-32 in my pocket and made for the fire exit. Banging the handle down, I was soon outside and standing on a sort of veranda. In front of me lay a car park. I made a quick decision to cross to the other side and look for a way out over there. If there wasn't an exit for cars, there was bound to be one for pedestrians. And it was the direction in which the District Line station lay, according to the lad on the checkout.

A short flight of steps led down to the asphalt. Trying to take them in one, I misjudged my landing and hit my knee on the ground. It didn't put me out of action, but it slowed me up as I made my way between the rows of cars.

'Stand still! Police!' The shout boomed across the car park from behind me.

'Don't move!' A different voice. I adjusted my mask, turned to face them and squinted through the eyeholes. There were three figures on the veranda. One was the officer who'd seen me coming out of the shop. Next to him, another officer was holding his two-way radio to his ear. The third figure was the shop assistant.

'Get on the ground right now!'

'Stay where you are!'

'Don't move!'

'Lie on the ground with your arms out – now!'

161

18

I've always liked commuting. That was why I went along with Clarissa's insistence on living in rural Essex, even though I had to travel into the City every day. When you're at home, your time belongs to your family. When you're at work, it belongs to your employer. When you're commuting, it belongs to you.

The old feeling of being as free as a bird returned as the District Line train rattled towards central London. I wasn't worried in the least. That might seem strange. But crowds were getting on and off at every stop, so I suppose it was safety in numbers. No one notices you on a busy Tube train. You leave your identity behind when you join the heaving mass of humanity.

The police hadn't come racing after me. It must have been because they knew I had a gun. The shop assistant would have told them. While they stood on the veranda calling up support, I was scaling the fence at the back of the car park. I landed on the soft earth of a flower bed in someone's back garden. To my left, a tree was shedding its leaves on a soggy lawn. To my right, a kiddies' slide stood rusty and abandoned. But in front of me I could see a path. It ran along the side of the house and looked like a way out. I followed it to the front garden, then through the front garden to a road. From there I could see the Underground station. It was off a little roundabout, no more than fifty yards away. My knee was giving me hell and I had developed a pain in my side. But I managed to get as far as the booking hall without encountering a single police officer.

By the time the train reached Plaistow, it was standing room only. I wondered what my fellow passengers would do if they knew I had a loaded gun on me. Janet had been right – it was easy to conceal. The pocket of my jeans showed hardly a bulge. The PK-32 was in a different league to the gun Rick had tossed in my lap. His weapon was twice the size and ten times as ugly. Unfortunately for him, I'd left it on the passenger seat when I jumped out of his car. He must have had a tough time explaining that one away.

Back at Johnson Terrace, there was a *To Let* sign outside number 14 and a van parked next to my Volvo. The van had *Painter and Decorator* on the side in fancy letters. Ma Drury was standing next to it, talking to a man in paint-stained overalls. Dressed in a plastic apron and rubber gloves, she looked as if she'd been cleaning Doug and Conrad's flat. The door to it was open. She stopped talking the moment she saw me.

'Someone's been asking for you,' she said as I limped up to her. 'A young woman. She came to the office and said she'd tried your flat. She wanted to know where you were. I said I didn't have a clue. I wouldn't have told her, anyway. We don't give out private information about our tenants.'

'Did she say who she was?'

Ma shook her head.

I wondered if it was Janet. 'What did she look like?'

The painter and decorator started showing an interest in our conversation.

'About thirty,' Ma said. 'Five-foot-six or so.' She thought for a while. 'Ordinary looking.'

That didn't sound like Janet. But I had to be sure. 'Was she wearing lipstick?'

Ma seemed surprised at the question. 'No ... no, she didn't have any lipstick,' she said after a long hesitation.

'Not a dark grey one?'

'No.'

'Hair?'

The painter and decorator was grinning.

Ma was getting irritated. 'Dark,' she said.

'I can't place her. What did she want?'

'She said you'd know right enough.'

The painter and decorator laughed. 'You're in trouble, mate,' he said. 'Looks like she's finally tracked you down, if you ask me.'

I hadn't asked him.

'Scarper,' he said. 'Could prove expensive if you don't.'

'What goes around comes around,' I said and got out my door keys.

The smell of damp in the hall was almost welcoming. I sorted through the mail on the floor, left George's pile outside his door and went upstairs with mine.

What am I supposed to do now? I asked myself the moment I got inside my flat. I was in possession of an illegal firearm. Drawing the bolts on my newly mended door, I pulled the gun out of my pocket and placed it on the table. It looked too small to be lethal. But it was enough to send me to prison. I searched the flat for a hiding place, finally discovering a loose floorboard. The gun went under there. I could decide what to do with it later.

There wasn't much mail. The local vicar had sent me his monthly newsletter – I didn't know where the church was. The kebab shop in the high street had sent me its menu – I'd never used it, and didn't intend to start. There was a leaflet from the council – the bin collection timetable. All addressed to 'The Occupier', except for a white envelope addressed to T. QUIRK without the E. It didn't have a stamp on it. I slit it open.

DEAR MR QUIRK
PHONE MONDAY 20th 5 TO 6 PM ASK FOR
DOREEN I WAS A FRIEND OF DOUGGIE
HAMILTON I HAVE SOMETHING TO TELL
YOU

At the bottom was a London phone number.

I wondered if it was from the dark-haired woman Ma Drury had told me about. If so, she must have put it through the letterbox when I didn't answer the door. I hadn't the faintest idea who she could be – I didn't know any Doreens. There was no demand for money, but one was sure to follow. Someone was on the make.

Around four o'clock I phoned Phil in California. He was breakfasting at a hotel in Sherman Oaks.

'This is to keep you in the loop,' I said. 'A lot has happened since we last spoke. You'll be surprised.'

'So surprise me,' he said.

I started by telling him about the visit from Vilday's enforcers. 'Bloody hell,' Phil burst out, 'it didn't take him long to get to you, did it? You poor bugger.'

'It's the jungle drums. I should have kept my mouth shut. Everyone around here knows everyone else's business. I should have realised that sooner.'

'Listen up, Tony, it's not worth it. I don't want this to end in your funeral – we're in a different ball park now. Leave Vilday out of it. We can write some episodes for my TV series. Don't worry, you'll still get your sixty per cent.'

'Sixty-five, you said.'

'Did I? I don't remember. If you say so, my old mucker, I suppose I must have. OK, sixty-five. But that's beside the point. Steer clear of Vilday. Neither of us will get a penny if you end up hors de combat.'

'I'm not giving up on Vilday yet,' I said. 'But there's more to come.'

Phil whistled incredulously when I told him about my run-in with Rick and Janet in her flat. He gave an ear-splitting 'Never!' when I told him how Rick had taught me to use the PK-32. The plan to assassinate Vilday in the Tied Struggler, and how I'd managed to get out of it, produced a long silence. It takes a lot to silence Phil. When at last he spoke it was to say, 'You're in it too deep, my son. Pull out before it's too late.'

'There's the book to think about,' I said. 'We mustn't forget the book.'

'Really? Is that the most important thing right now?'

'I want to finish it. There's a few more lines that I need to follow up.'

'Such as?'

'How Doug Hamilton got involved with Vilday, for a start.'

'Is that wise?'

I told Phil about the letter from Doreen.

'Doesn't sound genuine to me,' he said.

'It's worth a phone call to find out. Even if she only knew Doug slightly, it could be useful. We're writing a book about his murder but we know very little about him.'

'It's up to you,' Phil said. 'But I'll be surprised if anything comes of it.'

That remained to be seen. After ending the call, I went for a walk in the gathering dusk. Turning towards the river, I made my way through the warren of little streets until I reached the flood defences. For reasons I could only partly understand, I needed to let my eyes roam the length and breadth of the estuary. Maybe it was to lose myself in its emptiness. The way Janet had turned on me was affecting me more than I was willing to admit, least of all to Phil.

The flood defence wall was too high to see over, but I found a walkway which led to a block of council flats. I climbed the steps until the broad grey sweep of water came into view. A dark shape, identifying itself in the gloom only by its navigation lights, slipped noiselessly past. Upstream, the road bridge scored a barely discernible line across the river, its traffic silenced by the stiff wind that was blowing from the east. I leaned against the railings, gave myself up to the vastness of the estuary and felt the tension drain out of me. What wouldn't leave me was the horror. I could hardly believe what Janet and her messed-up friend had wanted me to do.

I couldn't get my head round it. Perhaps Phil was right. I was in too deep. It was only luck that had enabled me to escape. There wasn't the slightest possibility that Rick would have been waiting for me outside the Struggler when I emerged with blood on my hands. He would have gone to meet Janet at the airport. By the time the police caught up with me, they would have been winging their way to their bolt hole in the sun.

Whoever Rick was, he seemed to have established a Svengali-like control over Janet. He was the one to blame, not her. The tragedy had left her vulnerable and he'd taken advantage. She needed help, proper help. But as a source of information, I had to accept that she was finished. Could we write the book without her? I wasn't sure. A lot would depend on what Doreen had to say.

Monday the twentieth. I wasn't sure whether Doreen's note meant 'call between five and six' or 'call at five minutes before six'. The latter, I decided.

The phone rang a long time before it was answered.

'Yes?' A man's voice. There was music in the background. The Beach Boys.

'Can I speak to Doreen, please?'

'Who?'

'Sorry to bother you,' I said. 'I was told to ring this number and ask for Doreen.'

'Hang on, I'll find out for you.'

There was a clunk as the receiver went down. The music changed to country. A door banged. I could hear voices in the distance, young people's voices. It sounded as if the phone was in a pub.

'Hello?' A woman had picked up the receiver.

'Is that Doreen?' I said.

'Who wants her?'

'Tony Quirke. I got your letter.'

'Oh ... right.' The accent was Irish.

'You've something to tell me?'

'Yeah. About Douggie Hamilton.'

'I'm interested in what happened to him,' I said.

'I don't think they got the right man for it.'

'I don't either. Who do you think did it?'

No reply.

I waited. 'But you've got a good idea, haven't you?' I said. 'That's why you pushed that envelope through my letterbox.'

'One minute.' The receiver went down. The country singer held a high note. The door banged a couple of times, then there was silence. I got the impression that Doreen was on duty somewhere.

Several minutes passed. I was about to ring off when she came on the line again. 'I've got a name for you,' she said, the Irish accent thicker than ever, 'and I've got enough information to put him away for good. But I'm worried. It's the thought of him finding out.'

That sounded like Vilday. 'What was his connection with Doug?' I said.

'That would be telling.'

She was getting round to asking for money. 'I need to know,' I said.

'Are you going to make me an offer?'

Now we're getting somewhere, I thought. 'Three hundred?'

'Done,' she said, far too quickly. If she had anything worth knowing, she would have haggled.

'But it depends on what you've got.'

'Papers,' she said. 'Let's meet so I can show you. You can make up your mind then.'

My instinct was to say no, but I said, 'OK, meet where?'

'Odette's Kitchen?'

'What's that?'

'A bistro in Dagenham. On Lloyds Way, between Ernest Jones and Next. Do you know Lloyds Way?'

'No, but I can find it.'

'I could meet you there tonight,' she said. 'Eight o'clock?'

'I'll be there.'

19

Before I set out, I'd taken the trouble of satisfying myself that Odette's Kitchen was a genuine eatery. The photos on its website showed a long, low-ceilinged room divided into cosy alcoves that looked just right for a confidential chat. *A relaxed atmosphere*, one of the online reviews said. *Tough to choose from such a great menu, decided to go with the bouillabaisse. The best I've ever had. My only small criticism is that service is a little slow, but don't let that put you off.*

It didn't. I arrived at Lloyds Way in good time and had no difficulty finding Odette's Kitchen. Apart from the till on the reception desk, entering it was like going into someone's home. There were pictures on the walls and a freestanding stove in the middle of the dining area. I walked all the way through, glancing into the alcoves as I went. The only customers were a group of three young men dining with a woman who had spiky orange hair. She didn't match Ma's description of Doreen and she didn't seem to be looking out for anyone. I found myself a seat near the entrance. From there, I could see everybody who came in.

A waitress appeared and handed me a menu.

'I'm waiting for a friend,' I said and ordered a drink.

It was only five to eight, so I wasn't concerned that Doreen hadn't put in an appearance. I spent a few minutes studying the menu. After I'd decided I wasn't hungry, I occupied myself searching for divorce lawyers on the internet.

At exactly eight o'clock, I was interrupted by a cold blast of air that accompanied the opening of the door. A woman in her late thirties or early forties had come in. She wore a long green raincoat and a silver band across her dark hair. She was tall, around five-foot-eight. Letting the door swing shut behind her, she went to the reception desk and stood there waiting.

I rose from my seat. 'Doreen?'

All I got was a blank look before she turned her head away. It was only then that I noticed the blurred figure reaching for the door handle outside the restaurant. It was her companion for the evening. He joined her and they walked past me to their seats, the woman's heels clacking scornfully on the polished wooden floor. I went back to looking for divorce lawyers.

A quarter of an hour passed. Was this a hoax? Or had Doreen decided that meeting me wasn't worth the risk of provoking Vilday? Twice waitresses asked if I was ready to order. Twice I declined. I phoned the London number Doreen had given me but no one answered. At half past, tired of the staff's distrustful stares, I concluded that I'd been stood up. The restaurant was almost full, the buzz of conversation had risen to a deafening level and I'd finished my drink. I was about to walk out when yet another waitress came up to me.

'Mr Quirke?'

Surprised that she knew my name, I said, 'Yes?'

'Telephone message for you.' She glanced at her order pad. 'You're to go to 19A Truth Lane.'

I looked at her. 'Truth Lane? Where's that?'

She shook her head.

'OK,' I said. 'Truth Lane.' I got out my phone and opened the maps app. No luck. There wasn't a Truth Lane. Not in Dagenham, not in the whole of England. The only Truth Lane that came up was in Pennsylvania.

Had I heard her correctly? The waitress had disappeared, so I went to the reception desk and spoke to the waiter behind the till. 'I've just been given a message,' I said. 'Can I check the details with the waitress who gave it to me?'

He didn't seem to understand what I was saying.

'My name's Quirke,' I said. 'Someone took a phone message for me. I'd like to speak to the person who took it.'

'Sir?'

'Look,' I said, aware that the minutes were ticking away, 'this is important. Very important, actually.' Then I saw the waitress coming out of the kitchen with an order. 'That's her,' I said.

The waiter waved her over. She came as soon as she'd finished serving and stood in front of me looking uncomfortable. She must have thought I was making a complaint.

I asked her if she could repeat the message she'd given me.

'You had to go somewhere...' Her voice tailed off and she blushed.

'Was it you who took the call?' I said.

She nodded.

'You wrote it down,' I reminded her.

Her blush got even deeper. 'Yes, but...' After searching the pockets of her apron, she produced a crumpled piece of paper and handed it over.

'I'm sorry to trouble you,' I said, but she was walking away.

The waiter had decided I wasn't a valued customer. Slipping out from behind the till, he gripped my arm firmly above the elbow and propelled me towards the door. 'If sir isn't going to have a meal...'

I didn't want to create a scene.

The shops on Lloyds Way were closed and there weren't many pedestrians around, although there was still a lot of traffic. Standing in the light of Ernest Jones' shop window, I smoothed out the slip of paper and read it.

Mr Quirk 19A Truth Lane

So I'd heard correctly. My first thought was the flat. Had Doreen sent me to Dagenham to get me out of the way?

The new door was stronger than the previous one and it had a good lock, but there was no knowing what could happen if I wasn't there. My notes were all over the table. I didn't want them to vanish. There was also my CD collection.

The Volvo was parked about five minutes away, down a road on the other side of Lloyds Way. Keen to get back, I set off at a brisk pace past the shops. At the crossing I pressed the button and waited. Just then, something made me look over my shoulder. As I did, the headlights of an approaching van lit up a road sign on a wall behind me. *Tooth Lane.*

It was the waitress who'd heard it wrong.

Tooth Lane was a narrow cobbled passageway that ran between two office buildings. I followed it for about thirty yards to where it turned sharp right. From there it stretched a long way into darkness. On my right, the backs of the Lloyds Way shops soared like cliffs, scarred with filled-in windows and rusty wall anchors. On my left, the lane was bordered by a brick wall with barbed wire along the top. The only light was the glow from whatever lay on the other side of this wall.

Number 19A was the first of two terraced houses at the far end, both crying out for demolition. A few yards beyond them the lane was fenced off by wire mesh. A metal notice on the wire said *Warning! Construction Site – Keep Out!*

At first, I thought that 19A might be occupied because an overturned wheelie bin lay on the pavement outside. I rapped on the door with my knuckles – there wasn't a knocker or a bell. No response. I peered through the downstairs window. No lights were on inside. But even if there had been, it would have been difficult to see much. The glass was covered with a thick layer of grime. The place hadn't been lived in for years.

Realising that this could be a set-up, I looked behind me. The lane was deserted. I set off back the way I'd come, once more concerned about what was happening at my flat. But I had only gone a few yards before the lane entrance lit up with the headlights of an approaching car. It turned the corner and drove towards me on full beam. Blinded, I covered my eyes. Hello, Doreen. The car stopped about thirty yards away and didn't dip its lights. That could only mean one thing.

20

I had already pulled the wheelie bin upright and was crouching behind it when Doreen got off her first shot. It went straight through the bin and hit the wire fence behind me with a *ping!* So this was what she wanted to see me about.

In situations like that, you run on automatic. One moment I was cowering behind the wheelie bin, trying to make myself as small as possible, next moment I had the PK-32 in my hand. Sticking my head round the edge of the bin, I aimed at the nearest headlight and pulled the trigger. Nothing happened. I couldn't believe it. The magazine was full. I was still wondering what had gone wrong when Doreen's second shot went buzzing past my head.

Ducking behind the wheelie bin again, I stared at the PK-32 for a couple of crucial seconds before realising what the problem was. There was nothing up the spout. Rick's words came back to me. *To load the chamber for the first shot, you have to pull the slide back.*

I pulled it back, stuck my head out again and got off a hurried shot. The bullet went *pang!* into metal but the headlight stayed on. I fired again. That shot didn't even hit the car.

When Doreen fired a third time, I was making for the brick wall on the other side of the lane, dragging the wheelie bin alongside me as a shield. Even though I was still caught in the headlights, that shot missed me too. It didn't even hit the bin. As Rick could have told her, shooting at a moving target is difficult.

The wheelie bin thumped against the brick wall and I abandoned it. The only option now was forward, so I ran into the gap between the wall and the car. That plunged me into deep shadow and put the car between Doreen and me. She was standing beside the open driver-side door, staring into the darkness, trying to locate me. Everything seemed unreal. I wondered if I could make a dash for it, along Tooth Lane and on to Lloyds Way. But it was too far. Doreen could have brought me down before I'd gone ten yards.

It's difficult the first time you top someone. But don't think you haven't got the capacity. Everyone has. It's just a matter of bringing it out in you.

My pulse raced as I stretched my arms across the roof of the car. I was holding the PK-32 in both hands, the way Rick had taught me. Silhouetted in the reflected glare of the headlights, Doreen made a perfect target. My first shot had been a wild one, the second even wilder. This one would be straight out of the textbook.

There are two sights on a handgun, one at the front of the barrel and one at the rear.

Line the front sight with the target.

Then cover it with the rear sight.

Keeping the front sight on the target, breathe out slowly then squeeze the trigger.

Given the height of the car, my only option was a head shot. By now Doreen was looking straight at me, levelling her gun. But I was the first to squeeze my trigger. *Whack!* It was a shot Rick would have been proud of. Doreen's head jerked back and she disappeared from view.

Time stood still.

All I could hear was the gentle chugging of the engine. I called out, 'Are you all right?' It was a stupid thing to say, but I was numb with fright and the words just spoke themselves.

There was no reply.

It was unnerving, creeping round the car to where Doreen lay. I moved forward in a gunman's crouch, PK-32 at the ready, like a cop in a gangster movie. I was in a state of shock. I had never fired a pistol at anyone in my life, never mind a woman. But I had an even greater shock when I saw Doreen's body. Because it was the body of a man.

He lay on his back with his arms out, his gun a few feet away. I knelt down beside him. There was a hole in his forehead, fragments of bone on the cobbles and a spreading pool of blood. Any attempt at resuscitation would have been futile.

A vein in my temple started to throb. I took a closer look and realised that I'd seen him before. The broken nose, the scars on the chin and the clear blue eyes were terrifyingly familiar. The man I'd killed was one of the heavies who'd broken into my flat and given me a kicking. The bald one, the man in his sixties or seventies, the one who'd told me to stop asking questions. Vilday's enforcer. I nearly threw up.

21

I woke late, around midday. My clothes were scattered across the floor where I'd pulled them off. The bottle I'd emptied before I fell into bed lay on its side. The contents of my pockets were piled on a chair. Wallet, coins, keys, Doreen's letter. And on top of the pile, the Kofler PK-32.

Seeing it gave me the jitters. On the drive from Dagenham to Riverwell I'd done everything possible to avoid getting caught. I'd stuck to the speed limit in case a patrolling police car felt the need to pull me over. I'd taken B roads and a detour through Purfleet to avoid as many number plate cameras as possible. When I got to Johnson Terrace, I'd even waited until the street was clear before entering number 12. And after all that, I'd left the PK-32 beside my bed in plain sight.

Leaping out of bed, I put it back in its hidey-hole

under the loose floorboard. Still worried, I dragged the wardrobe a couple of feet sideways to hold the floorboard down. There wasn't much more I could do. Not for the time being.

It was difficult, getting a grip on my nerves. I couldn't take my mind off what would be happening in Tooth Lane. I could see the white-suited scene of crime officers as clearly as if I was standing next to them. They'd be everywhere, crouching beside the body, photographing it, carrying out fingertip searches, picking up fragments of bone and putting them into evidence bags. And when they'd found the bullets, they'd send them off to be examined for rifling marks. Marks that could connect them to the gun.

Did the PK-32 have rifling? I seemed to recall Rick saying that handguns often don't. I dragged the wardrobe off the loose floorboard again. After squinting down the barrel, I wasn't sure. I stood next to the window to get a better look. I still wasn't sure. Then I remembered that the firing chamber reloaded after every shot. I was staring down the barrel at a live round. I put the PK-32 away pretty quick after that.

Rifling marks were only part of my problem. There was also the question of the cartridge cases. Like a fool, I hadn't thought to pick them up. Three of them on the cobbles, two outside 19A and one between the car and the wall. I looked at my watch. It was ten past twelve. They would have been found by now. There wouldn't be any DNA on them because Rick had worn gloves when he loaded the magazine. I hadn't touched them either. But

I remembered what the gun expert had said at Conrad's trial. *When a gun is fired, it leaves tiny impressions on the cartridge case. We call these ballistic fingerprints. They're like fingerprints because they can identify the gun that made them.*

I hadn't touched the cartridge cases – but I'd left fingerprints on them. Fingerprints that could sink me.

'Don't beat yourself up. It could have been you lying dead on the ground, not him.'

It was that evening. I was sitting in Phil's living room in Putney drinking his whisky, working my way into the biggest hangover of my life. Phil had got back from the States a few hours earlier and hadn't unpacked yet. He was perched on the edge of a chair, leaning forward with his elbows on his knees, studying me intently. I couldn't bring myself to return his gaze. I could only stare into the bottom of my glass, as if it contained a solution to the mess I was in.

'What do you want me to do?' Phil asked for the umpteenth time.

For the umpteenth time, I didn't reply.

'We can make sure they don't pin it on you,' he said. 'It's mainly a matter of disposing of the gun.' He stood up, went to the window and looked out. He seemed to expect hordes of police to be assembling on the pavement outside. 'I should never have let you go after Vilday,' he said. 'And I should have insisted on ignoring that odious woman's letter.'

'There was no way I could have run for it,' I said. 'I had to shoot him or he would have shot me.'

'Of course. Anyone in that situation would have done the same.'

'I think I'd better call the police,' I said.

Phil turned away from the window. 'Do you want to go to prison? Is that the plan?'

'I have to report it,' I said.

'You don't have to do any such thing. The problem is not of your making. You got a letter, the letter said let's meet, you went along in good faith, you were ambushed. It was a trap.'

'I still want to hand myself in. I acted in self-defence. When I explain that to the police, they'll understand. They'll have to.'

'That would be the biggest mistake of your life,' Phil said. 'Do you think you'd get a fair hearing?'

I thought of Conrad's jury. Then I thought of Ursula Jolliffe. The look on my face must have answered Phil's question.

'Well then,' he said, looking out of the window again, 'You'd better lie low for a while. You're welcome to move in here. Until you find somewhere new, that is. If you'll excuse the primitive arrangements.'

Primitive? By any standard, Phil's flat was classy. There was only one bedroom, but the living room was comfortable and there was a sofa for me to sleep on. The utility room was fully equipped, as was the dining kitchen. To make it even classier, there was a terraced garden which Phil shared with his well-to-do neighbours.

I spent the night on his sofa, but I couldn't get to sleep. Phil had insisted on watching the TV news that evening. Inevitably, it had included an item on Tooth Lane. The police were calling it a gangland assassination, which pleased Phil because it meant they were following the wrong trail. For me, it only brought back sights and sounds I'd been trying to forget.

All night my senses ran on overdrive, as if I was still scrambling out of the gunman's line of fire. I felt the PK-32 kick in my hand. I saw gunsmoke drift along the roof of the car, then fade into nothing. I saw clear blue eyes stare lifelessly over my shoulder into the night sky. I saw blood draw grotesque patterns as it trickled along the grooves between the cobbles.

He was out to kill you. You had no choice. It was the only way you could save your life. It was him or you.

Around midnight, I got out my phone and googled criminal defence lawyers. *It is not an offence to use reasonable force to protect yourself from serious injury or death*, one of the websites said. *If you act instinctively in the heat of the moment, that is enough to ensure that you are acting lawfully and in self-defence.*

Instinctively? In the heat of the moment? I'd stretched out my arms and taken careful aim at what I thought was Doreen's head. That shot had been *calculated*. I would never have believed myself capable of doing such a thing. But I'd proved myself capable, and I'd done it, and someone had died.

I spent the rest of that sleepless night thinking about the dead man. Did he have a family? A wife? Brothers and sisters? Children? I wanted to know – and I didn't want to know. It's a strange relationship you have with a man you've killed. It's almost spiritual. After he's gone you don't hate him any more, no matter what he was trying to do to you. You want to get close to him, closer than to anyone else in the world. Especially when you don't even know his name.

22

As soon as the Drury Properties office opened next morning, I phoned Ma and told her I was going away for a while. I wanted to keep the Johnson Terrace flat, I said. I would have ended the tenancy there and then, but there wasn't room in Phil's flat for all my stuff. It would have to stay in number 12 until I found somewhere permanent.

My hangover hadn't worn off by the time I drove to Riverwell that afternoon, paid the next month's rent and came away with a few essentials. These included the PK-32. I didn't want to leave it in the flat. Phil was urging me to take a trip to the other side of London and drop it in a litter bin when no one was watching. But I had decided to hang on to it. I could only assume that Vilday still had me in his sights.

Knowing how close I'd come to disaster, Phil renewed

his efforts to persuade me to give up. 'You'd be a fool to take any more risks,' he said over supper that evening.

'Are you sure you're not underestimating me?' I replied.

Phil looked up from the spaghetti bolognese I'd cooked for him and gave me an encouraging smile. 'I would never underestimate you, Tony.'

'I know what I want,' I said.

'Yes,' he said. 'You know what you want. Tell me – what is it?'

'Janet and Rick were right. Vilday needs taking out.'

Phil looked worried.

'No,' I said, 'not like that. I'm going to do it the legal way, before he succeeds in taking me out.'

'You're going to cross swords with Vilday again? Is that wise?'

Deep down, Phil wanted me to do it. I could tell. He was a writer, and like all writers, constantly on the lookout for a good plot. Vilday would make one hell of a villain, that was for sure.

'He'll never trace me to Putney,' I said. 'When the police have arrested him, I'll get out of your hair and find a place of my own.'

Phil looked thoughtful. 'You're rubbing shoulders with scumbags. I would hate to see you ending up like one of them.'

'There's no chance of that,' I said.

'OK,' he said quickly, 'if you insist. Let's bust him. So what do we do next?'

'Follow the money,' I said.

According to Miss Prim, shortly before Doug was murdered he'd come into a heap of cash, enough to think of buying a sports car. She'd assumed he'd made it from selling paintings. I wondered exactly how much his art had earned him, so next day I got in touch with the gallery.

'Good morning, Willoughby Gallery.' There was a touch of Cockney beneath the cut-glass vowels.

'I believe you have some paintings by Douglas Hamilton.'

'Just a minute, sir,' the woman said. 'Douglas Hamilton … yes, we do. How can I help?'

'I saw three of them on your website. Carnations, spring flowers and a … a kingfisher, I believe. Are they still for sale?'

'Oh yes, sir. Everything on our website is for sale. You can buy online or on the premises. Would you like me to arrange a viewing?'

'That depends,' I said. 'Do you have any other works by Hamilton?'

'I'll check for you.'

It was a long time before she picked up the phone again. 'I'm sorry, sir. Those are the only Hamilton pieces we have.'

'You must have sold a lot, then.'

'Excuse me?'

'Put it this way. Have Hamiltons been flying off the shelves?'

'I'm sure you'll find they're a good investment, sir.' The receptionist was beginning to sound frosty. 'If you would like advice on the state of the market, may I suggest—'

'Can't you just tell me how many you've sold?'

There was a sharp intake of breath.

'It would be nice to know,' I said. 'If I'm going to spend a lot of money on one.'

The receptionist must have remembered that the customer is always right. 'I'll check that for you, sir. One minute, please.'

There was another long wait. Then, 'We don't appear to have sold any.'

'None?'

'The three on our website are the only paintings Mr Hamilton left with us, sir. Would you like me to arrange a viewing?'

'I'll have to discuss that with my partner,' I said.

'Perhaps I should mention we have a ten per cent discount on sales until next Friday.'

'Then we'll have to get a move on, won't we?'

'Doug's money didn't come from selling paintings,' I said to Phil. 'Not one penny. That tells us a lot.'

'Are you saying you've cracked it?' Phil replied.

'He must have got it from selling drugs,' I said. 'I should have paid more attention to what Janet told me. She said he was into drugs, and Brayne-Thompson even said that Vilday was supplying him. The murder's got to be drug-related. All of a sudden Doug was in the money, then he was killed. That's got drugs written all over it. It's the line we should have been following from the start. Let me hazard a guess. Vilday had taken on Doug as a runner.

They fell out over something. Maybe Doug owed Vilday money and refused to hand it over. Maybe he wanted to spend it on the car Miss Prim told me about. Whatever the reason, Vilday did what he does to people who cross him.'

Phil thought about it. 'And your evidence is?'

'I haven't got any,' I said. 'But someone must know something.'

Phil leaned back with his hands behind his head and stared at the ceiling. 'What did Janet tell you about Doug?'

I thought about the meetings I'd had with her. 'To be honest, very little.'

'If you approached her nicely, do you think she'd—'

I laughed out loud. 'Are you serious?'

There was a grin on Phil's face. He has a sense of humour, but sometimes he takes it too far. 'I was wondering how long that little love affair would last,' he said.

He went into his bedroom and came back with his laptop. 'Let's get down to it.' He googled for a few minutes, then found what he was looking for. 'Here you are,' he said, and read it out. '*Police were called to the property on Saturday morning where they found 29-year-old Douglas Hamilton's body.* Let's see … let's see … *Conrad Connor, also 29, who shared the flat* … Ah – here's the thing. *Connor's father Shaun, speaking to reporters at Hadgate House, his care home in Exeter, said, "This is not our Conrad. Conrad is a decent young man, he'd never do anything like that. The police have made a big mistake …"*'

Phil turned the laptop round to show me a press photo of an old man in a high-backed armchair. Shaun Connor, the caption said. Conrad's dad. A harmless senior citizen whose life had been ruined by a wrongful conviction.

'That's it,' I said. 'Mr Shaun Connor, Hadgate House, Exeter. He'll know all about Doug's extra-curricular activities.'

23

Hadgate House stood at the top of a steep hill some distance from St David's station. When I got out of the taxi, I was surprised by how shabby it looked. Several terraced houses had been knocked into one, not very spacious houses at that. Their white uPVC windows didn't go with the 1930s stained glass on the front door, and the conservatory tacked on the end was long past its prime. I wouldn't have wanted to spend the last years of my own life there.

After checking in at reception, a care assistant led me along a narrow corridor to a room with *Mr S. Connor* on the door. She knocked loudly and ushered me in.

'Here's Mr Quirke, all the way from London to see you, darling,' she said.

It was a smallish room with not much furniture. Mr Connor was sitting in an armchair with his back to me, facing the window. All I could see of him was the top of his head, strands of thin grey hair shining under the harsh glare of the ceiling light. He showed no sign of having heard us enter.

'Mr Connor,' the care assistant said more loudly.

I couldn't help noticing the collection of family photos. They were propped up around a white plastic crucifix on a shelf above the radiator. I looked at them while the care assistant bent over Mr Connor and gently woke him up. One was of a young man on a quayside with sailboats in the background. It was Conrad, jollier and more self-assured than the Conrad I'd seen in the dock at the Crown Court. Another showed a couple in the portico of a church, presumably Mr Connor senior and Mrs Connor. The third was a young woman with mousy hair – Janet, before she discovered blonde hair dye and grey lipstick.

'Chaffinch!' Mr Connor exclaimed, leaning forward to point a finger at the window. The garden outside was glorious with autumn colours. Even the clouds had parted to let a little sun through. It was so peaceful I almost forgot the reason I'd come.

'Yes, darling, a chaffinch,' the care assistant said without looking. 'Mr Connor does so love his birds,' she said in an aside to me. 'Would you like some tea, Mr Connor? Tea and choccy biccies? How about you, Mr Quirke?'

Mr Connor didn't reply, so I said, 'No, thanks.'

As soon as the care assistant left us alone, I dragged a chair to the window and sat facing him. Mr Connor studied me silently for a few moments in that slightly mistrustful way old people have, then licked his thin lips and put out his hand. We shook as if we were old friends.

'Good to meet you, Mr Connor,' I said, looking into dark brown eyes as alert as any sixteen-year-old's. Before I arrived at Hadgate House, I had no way of knowing whether he suffered from dementia. The care home wouldn't tell me when I phoned to arrange the visit, so I could have been wasting my time, but it seemed that I was in luck. Once he got going, Mr Connor was as bright as a berry.

'They told me you knew Conrad,' he said.

'Only a little,' I replied. 'I'd like to know more about him. And about his flatmate Doug.'

Suspicion clouded the old man's face. 'Are you a reporter? Because if you are—'

'I promise you, I'm not a reporter.'

'—you can get out right now. What they said about Conrad wasn't true. They shouldn't be allowed to print things like that.' Mr Connor was angry, and we'd hardly started.

'I didn't know Conrad well,' I said, 'but I do count myself a friend. I was as shocked as everybody else when it happened.'

'It was what she read in the papers that did for Nora,' Mr Connor said. 'She had a stroke, you know. She can hardly move. They have to lift her in and out of bed on a hoist.' I gripped his hand to show how much I felt about his loss. There was a slight tremor that I hadn't noticed before.

'This terrible affair has caused me a great deal of pain,' I said.

'You've come all this way to tell me that?'

'No, Mr Connor. I'm convinced that your son was innocent, and I'm going to do all I can to clear his name. The evidence they used against him was weak. A lot of it was based on misunderstandings, and in my opinion, none of it was conclusive. I live next door to where Doug and Conrad had their flat, and I've made it my business to look into the case. I believe that Conrad was set up for a crime he did not commit. He was as much a victim as Doug. I want to go to the authorities. I want them to quash the verdict. And I want the newspapers to apologise for all the things they said about him.'

Mr Connor gave me another suspicious look, as if I was making fun of him. 'But why have you come to me?' he said.

'I'm here to ask your help, if you're prepared to give it.'

'I don't think there's much I could do to help—'

'No, Mr Connor, I'm not asking you to do anything,' I said. 'It's information I'm after.'

For a few moments we looked at each other. I wasn't sure what he saw in my face. But it must have persuaded him that I was sincere. 'If you think so,' he said.

'Let's get down to it, then. Does the name Vilday mean anything to you? Gregory Vilday?'

Mr Connor shook his head.

'He could have been one of Doug Hamilton's friends. Or an acquaintance. You're sure the name doesn't ring any bells?'

Mr Connor shook his head again. It was disappointing, but I had plenty more questions.

'Did Conrad ever mention anyone who had a grudge against Doug?'

Mr Connor looked blank.

'Do you think that Doug had anything to do with illegal drugs?' I said. 'Do you think he could have been dealing them?'

A note of indignation entered Mr Connor's voice. 'No – and Conrad didn't either. I'd have known. Neither of those boys ever did anything like that.'

It was a dead end. I decided to switch tracks. 'I wish I'd seen more of Conrad,' I said. 'I suppose you have a lot of happy memories of him.'

This was a much more productive line of enquiry. Phil had urged me to dig deep into Conrad's background. *We've got to make readers sympathise with him. Otherwise they won't feel angry when he's sold down the river by the court. The child is the father of the man, to coin a phrase. Conrad's story begins when he's learning to walk, yeah? So what can we put in the book about that?*

'What was he like as a toddler?' I said.

This got Mr Connor going. There were times when it was hard to get a word in edgeways. He told me about the early days when the Connor family – Shaun, Nora, Conrad and Janet – lived in Tilbury. In those days, Mr Connor ran a one-man window cleaning business. Theirs was an honest, decent working class family which it was only possible to admire.

Even though I'd drawn a blank on drugs, I was more

than glad I'd come. I was building a picture of Conrad Connor that was bound to please Phil and his even harder-to-please literary agent, Holly. As a child, Mr Connor told me, Conrad had been slow to speak and was backward at school. He left without qualifications, and Shaun and Nora were concerned about his future. Their concern was not misplaced. Conrad drifted from one dead-end job to another, and there were frequent periods of unemployment. But meeting Doug at the local college of further education was a turning point. Conrad had gone there for help with basic literacy and numeracy. Doug was taking a course in art. Doug's pictures sparked Conrad's interest in the subject, he signed on for an art course of his own and was soon painting away happily. He was so keen that when Mr and Mrs Connor retired and moved to Exeter, Conrad decided not to go with them. Instead, he moved into a flat with Doug – the infamous Flat 1 in 14 Johnson Terrace, Riverwell.

That was where Doug's mother, the formidable Theresa Hamilton, came into the picture. The divorced wife of a wealthy Leicestershire landowner, she did not approve of her son's relationship with Conrad. Before he turned to art, Doug had dropped out of agricultural college and spent several years drifting on the continent. According to Mr Connor, Mrs Hamilton saw Doug's relationship with Conrad as another step on the rocky path to ruin. I asked him to tell me everything he knew about her. It wasn't much. 'We weren't good enough for Mrs Hamilton' was how he summed it up. But perhaps that said it all.

'Would it have been better if Conrad had never met Doug?' I said. I was mindful of the crucifix on the shelf over the radiator, but I needn't have worried.

'I'd been hoping that Conrad would join me in the business,' Mr Connor said. 'Take it over one day. He gave it a go for a while, but he didn't like working out of doors. Up a ladder in the cold, that sort of thing. It was much nicer sitting in a warm studio painting pictures. But I respected his wishes and he had our blessing. Do I wish he'd never met Doug? No, Mr Quirke. It was Doug who gave him his confidence, Doug who made our Conrad believe in himself. He came into his own after that – it was wonderful to see.'

The more I listened to Mr Connor, the more I found myself liking him. His dignity, loyalty to his family and simple faith shone like a bright light in the murky world I had come to inhabit. It only strengthened my resolve to clear his son's name.

Worried that we might run out of time – they'd warned me at reception that Mr Connor might be wheeled away for a bath that afternoon – I turned to the delicate issue of Janet. I didn't want to mention her approach to me after the trial, or all that had followed. But I owed it to Mr Connor to tell him what a terrible state she was in. I had formed the impression that he didn't know how ill she was – so far, he hadn't mentioned her. But he had to be told, because I was convinced that she needed professional help.

'Is that your daughter?' I said, pointing to her photo on the shelf over the radiator.

Mr Connor twisted his head round. His armchair was still facing the window and he couldn't quite see. So I got up and brought the photo across for him.

There was a long silence as he looked at it.

'Yes,' he said. 'This is Janet.'

'Janet and Conrad,' I said. 'Were they close?'

Mr Connor lifted his eyes from the photo and looked at me with what I can only describe as despair. I was shocked at the sudden change the photo had brought about in him. I wondered if I had said something wrong.

'Yes,' he said, 'they were close.' Tears glistened in his eyes.

'She must have been a great comfort to you after the tragedy.'

'If only,' he said. 'How do you think I feel, Mr Quirke, now that both of my children are dead?'

There haven't been many times when I've felt that the Earth has stopped turning on its axis, but that was one of them.

'Janet *dead*? What do you mean?' For a moment I was afraid she'd taken her own life.

By now Mr Connor was sobbing. He made no attempt to dry his tears.

'It's not your fault,' he managed to gasp. 'You had no way of knowing. Janet was killed in a car crash a year ago next month.'

24

I stared out of the train window all the way to London and saw nothing. It wasn't because darkness had fallen or the view was obscured by rain – for most of the way, the sky was clear. It was because my mind was in a spin. The cleaners even had to turn me out of my seat when we arrived at Paddington.

At first, I thought that Mr Connor must be suffering from dementia after all, but ruled that out when I remembered how articulate he had been. So who was the woman who had run after me at the end of the trial? Could Janet have come back from the dead to avenge her brother? Perhaps, if you believe in ghosts – but I don't.

I was left with the only rational explanation. The woman who had said she was Janet Connor was someone else. Someone who, for whatever reason, had pretended to be Conrad's sister.

Even that raised more questions than it answered. If the woman who'd buttonholed me after the trial was not Conrad's sister, why would she want me to kill the man who'd committed the crime Conrad was sent to prison for? It didn't add up. Could she be Doug's sister? That would give her a bigger reason for seeking revenge. But why would Doug's sister pretend to be Janet Connor? And I knew from the trial that Doug Hamilton had been an only child.

I couldn't forget how Janet's voice had broken with emotion when she talked about Conrad's suicide. Even the most skilful actor could never have faked a performance like that. Could she have been his lover? But Conrad's only relationship had been with Doug, hadn't it? *Janet, Janet, Janet…* Her name went round inside my head for the whole of the journey. *Who are you?*

It was too complicated to explain to Phil over the phone. I waited until I got back to his flat. As the District Line train dawdled towards East Putney, I bet myself that when I told him, he'd come out with 'Somehow, I don't think we're in Kansas any more.' I lost my bet.

'How was your trip?' he asked the minute I walked in. 'A sensational triumph? Do we now know that Doug was dealing drugs for Vilday? And have you got Conrad's bio sorted? I hope you have, because we're on the move. You won't believe who I've been talking to.'

'OK,' I said. 'You tell me your news and then I'll tell you mine.'

Phil looked at the cans I'd bought on my way from the station. 'Give me one of those,' he said.

I handed him an interesting-looking craft beer from a south London microbrewery, one I'd never heard of before.

'I've been out for a drink with Holly,' Phil said, yanking off the tab and putting the can to his lips. 'Dear, darling, shoot-from-the-hip Holly, and – guess who? Guess who? None other than—'

He raised the can as if proposing a toast. 'Only Brenda Dutton, commissioning editor of Echo Press. Holly's sold her the book!' He threw himself on the sofa and grinned up at me. 'Almost sold it, anyway. But I've got a good feeling about this one. We haven't got a contract yet, but I'm a good judge of people, and I can tell you that Brenda Dutton wants to run with it. Oh Brenda, Brenda, I love you!'

'That's excellent news,' I said. 'But we need to talk. Seriously, I mean.'

'Fancy a Chinese?' he said. 'I think a celebration is in order.'

'Phil – there's something I have to tell you. Janet Connor isn't the person she says she is.'

He gave me a pitying look. 'Who is? I'm not the person I say I am. If you knew what I get up to when no one's around—' He burst out laughing. 'And I happen to know that Tony Quirke is not the person he says he is. Here's the thing, Tony – that's how literature works. Nobody's who they say they are. King Lear's not the big swinging dick he makes himself out to be at the start. Hamlet—'

'Janet Connor is dead!' I had to shout to get through to him. 'She died a year ago. The woman who wanted me to kill Vilday was someone else.'

Phil blinked a couple of times, then stared at me with his mouth open, gripping the can so hard he almost crushed it. 'Someone else?' he said. 'Are you telling me she's been having you on?'

'I'm not sure what I'm telling you.'

'What a bugger,' he said. 'According to Holly, Brenda's only interested in the book because you've been talking to Conrad's sister. Like Holly says, it's the source that sells the project. But now it appears that you haven't been talking to her. If that's what you're telling me, Tony, you're telling me we're fucked.'

'I'm sorry,' I said. 'She fooled me completely. She's a good actor.'

'I don't think she needed a lot of acting skills to fool a berk like you.'

Putney is good for eateries. Phil took me to a place off the high street where we ate Malaysian and I ran through my visit to Mr Connor. Our celebration had become a business meeting.

'Sort of changes things, doesn't it?' I said.

'We'll have to drill deeper,' Phil said. 'All we've seen so far is shadows on the wall, and it's not clear who's making them. First off, we need to find out who Janet really is.' His frown posed the question, how?

'Colin might help,' I said.

'Colin?'

'The retired detective. I should have thought of him sooner. Investigations are his thing.'

I phoned his number. It was answered by Mrs Christie.

'I'm sorry to bother you,' I said, 'but I wonder if I could have a word with Colin? Tony Quirke here—'

'Tony who?'

'Quirke. I'm the friend of Len Mackle's who dropped by the other day.'

No reply.

'I hope it's not inconvenient,' I said, 'but I was wondering if Colin – hello?'

The line had gone dead. She'd cut me off.

I phoned Len at the Swan in the hope of a more cordial reception. His voice was a breath of fresh air. 'Tony! Good to hear from you – I thought you'd deserted us for the Dog and Fox. What can I do for you?'

'I'm taking a little break,' I said, 'that's why I haven't been in recently. Away for a bit of R and R, you might say. But yes, there is something you can do for me. I went to see Colin Christie, as you suggested. He was very helpful, but now there seems to be a problem. I tried to phone him a few minutes ago and got a chilly reception from his wife. She didn't want me to speak to him. I hope I didn't overstay my welcome the first time.'

Len's voice became grave. 'You won't have heard, then. I'm sorry to have to tell you that Colin has passed on. Three days ago. The funeral's on Saturday.'

I couldn't think of anything to say.

'Colin was a legend,' Len continued. 'Relentless in his pursuit of the bad guys. God knows, we need plenty of people like Colin Christie around here.'

I promised Len I'd send a wreath and ended the call.

'Another blind alley?' said Phil.

'You could call it that. Colin's no longer with us.'

Phil pulled a face. 'We'll have to have a good excuse if we want to keep Holly onside.'

'Know any skip tracers?' I said.

He didn't.

I googled.

UNDERWOOD TRACING SERVICES
Simon Underwood, ex-Metropolitan Police,
Founder and Team Leader.
No Trace, No Fee.

'That's the one,' I said.

The offices of Underwood Tracing Services were on the third floor of a commercial block in Ilford. Turning off Ilford Hill, Phil followed the access road to a private car park and backed his Peugeot into an empty space. Inside the building, a receptionist rang through to the third floor, then sent us up in the lift.

Simon Underwood was waiting for us in the corridor. He was a tall, heavily built man of about sixty, thin on top with eyes that didn't look as if they missed much. As I was soon to discover, he was entirely without humour. He wasn't the sort of person you'd want to go on holiday with. But he was just the person to hire if you were seeking the identity of an imposter.

He ushered us into his tiny office and asked us to take a seat. As he eased his huge frame into the swivel chair behind his desk, I noticed how clear the desktop was. There were no documents, no in trays, no desk tidies, just a large expanse of teak veneer and a phone. The office was as bare as the desk – he had a computer and a printer at his elbow, and that was all. There wasn't even a filing cabinet. The only decoration on the walls was a framed certificate which said that Underwood Tracing Services was the Enquiry Agency of the Year. The date was three years previously.

'Basically,' I said, 'we need to know the identity of someone who's been operating under an alias.' I gave Underwood a heads-up on where things stood. I left a lot out. The attempt to get me to assassinate Vilday. The kicking I got from Vilday's heavies. The phone call from Doreen and the incident on Tooth Lane. I wasn't going to incriminate myself.

Underwood's eyes never left my face. When I told him about my meetings with Janet, they narrowed.

'Was it a close relationship?' he asked.

'What's a close relationship?' I replied.

Underwood leaned forward with his elbows on the desk and clasped his hands. 'A close relationship is when you've had sex three times,' he said.

'Oh no, there was nothing … nothing like that.'

Underwood's expression didn't change.

'I can't see what sex has got to do with it,' said Phil.

'It's usually got everything to do with it,' said Underwood.

I could tell that Phil's temper was beginning to fray. 'Fair enough,' he said, 'but all we want to know is who the hell she is.'

'She wanted you to get her brother off the hook?' Underwood said, looking at me. 'Even though he wasn't her brother?'

I nodded.

'Even though she knew you'd been a juror at his trial?'

'That's right.'

He shook his head. 'If you don't mind me saying, Mr Quirke, you'd be well advised to have nothing more to do with this young lady.'

'But can you find out who she is?' I said.

'Why do you want to know? Sounds like you're going to write a book about her.'

Phil laughed.

Underwood swung his chair round to face his computer, printed off his terms and conditions and handed them over. In the normal course of events, he explained, he could trace someone's whereabouts within forty-eight hours. But that was if he had a name to start with. We hadn't given him one.

'That's the whole point,' said Phil.

'I've got her address,' I said, 'if it's any use.' I gave him details of her flat in Aveley House.

'We'll take it from there, then,' Underwood said, in the deadpan manner I was getting used to.

I remembered something else. 'Her flat's got two parking spaces at the back.'

'That'll help.'

I noticed that he didn't write anything down. He seemed to carry everything in his head.

'This is what we'll do,' he said. 'We'll conduct a covert surveillance on Flat 507, compile a video log of who's going in and out, then show it to you. Once you've confirmed it's the woman you're interested in, we'll trace her identity and do our standard background search.'

The video surveillance would be a two-man job, he explained. Nothing illegal was involved, but it would push the price up. He pointed to the scale of charges on the list of terms and conditions.

'Can we afford it?' I whispered to Phil.

Underwood looked out of the window, pretending not to listen.

'Don't worry, I'll handle it,' Phil whispered back, then said, 'That's fine, Mr Underwood. It's exactly what we want. Please go straight ahead.'

25

Next day, Phil went to Newcastle to film the first episode of his TV series. It was too soon to expect anything from Underwood, so I decided to look into the identity of the Tooth Lane gunman. It was something I'd been avoiding. Tooth Lane was an episode in my life that was difficult to face up to. But I knew it had to be done sooner or later. The attacks were escalating. Vilday had made two attempts on me already, the second of which had nearly sent me to the crematorium. The third attempt might be the last.

I didn't have to search the internet for long.

MAN SHOT DEAD IN ALLEY MAY BE
VICTIM OF GANG WARFARE
A man was shot to death yards from busy Lloyds Way,
Dagenham, yesterday night. Although the body has

not been formally identified, police believe that he
was Brian Loughty, 67. He may have been targeted
in a tit-for-tat gangland execution, police have said.

He was found lying on the ground next to his blue
Ford Mondeo. A handgun was found nearby. Forensic
tests proved that it belonged to the dead man.

Detectives believe that the shooting occurred
four to eight hours before the body was discovered.
Loughty, known by his nickname 'Mad Brian', had
convictions for grievous bodily harm and extortion. If
he was targeted in a feud between warring criminal
gangs, his killer or killers...

Loughty? The name sounded familiar. Then it came back to me. What my googling had uncovered at Arthur Drury's funeral. Brian Loughty had been Arthur's sidekick before he went straight, the convict he'd shared a cell with in Belmarsh Prison. The one who'd helped him attack the prison officer. It was a shock to discover that Vilday's hitman had been one of Arthur Drury's friends. It brought Tooth Lane closer to home. But what did it tell me? Practically nothing. I already knew that Vilday was well in with the Druries. I could only conclude that Brian Loughty was another unconnected piece of information to add to the pile. Eventually, if I could collect enough pieces, they'd fit together into one big picture that would explain everything. That day seemed a very long way off.

My phone pinged with an incoming email.

Dear Mr Quirke,
CUSTOMER CONTRACT REFERENCE NO:
C001502
Occupant of Flat 507 Aveley House is using Bay 23
in Aveley House car park. Subject drives a Nissan
GT-R. Investigator followed subject into building,
saw her let herself into 507. Did not emerge for 2
hr 25 min, was followed to shops where she entered
M&S and surveillance terminated.

The email included a link to Underwood's website. I entered the password he had given us and watched a video clip of a woman getting out of a Nissan sports car. Surprisingly, it wasn't Janet. The woman in the clip was older, taller and had dark hair. The camera followed her through the car park to the Aveley House entrance. She didn't walk like Janet, either. She waddled. Janet had a more elegant way of walking.

Not Janet Connor, I emailed back. *Keep looking.*

Underwood's next email came through the following morning.

Dear Mr Quirke,
CUSTOMER CONTRACT REFERENCE NO:
C001502
Aveley House is owned by Amities Serviced
Apartments. The current tenant of Flat 507
is Maria Tsiolkas. Do you wish us to trace the

previous address of Maria Tsiolkas? The tenants
of 507 before Tsiolkas were Christopher and
Blanche Nudds. Do you wish us to trace the current
whereabouts of Christopher and Blanche Nudds?

Trace Mr and Mrs Nudds, I emailed back.

I had to kick my heels for a whole day before I received a reply. It was frustrating, to say the least.

> *Dear Mr Quirke,*
> *CUSTOMER CONTRACT REFERENCE NO:*
> *C001502*
> *Re: Christopher and Blanche Nudds*
> *Please contact this office for your interim report.*

By three thirty that afternoon, I was in the lift going up to Underwood's third-floor offices, annoyed that he hadn't emailed the report to me, or even made it available on his website. I found Simon Underwood perched on the corner of his desk, talking on the phone. He motioned for me to take a seat.

'We found out more than we expected,' he said when he'd ended his call. Keeping the receiver to his ear, he buzzed his secretary. 'Nancy, can Mr Quirke have a cup of tea, please? And are there any custard creams left?'

'What do you mean, found out more than you expected?' I said.

Underwood settled himself behind his desk. 'This is not our bag, Mr Quirke, not our bag. It's a case for the police. My professional advice is to leave it to them.' He swivelled his chair round and brought a document up on his screen.

'I think we told you that until recently Flat 507 was leased by a Christopher and Blanche Nudds,' he said. 'They're brother and sister. The young woman you're interested in could have been Blanche. Christopher terminated the lease last week and Miss Tsiolkas moved in the following day. Where the Nuddses went after that, I can't tell you. Not yet. But we're working on it.'

'What was the name again?' I said.

'The woman you're interested in? Blanche Nudds. B-L-A-N-C-H-E. It's all in the interim report. I'll print it out for you.'

'You said it's not your bag. What did you mean by that? And what have the police got to do with it?'

'It's your business, Mr Quirke,' Underwood said, 'but I wouldn't be doing my job if I didn't warn you. The Nuddses have previous. It's best to steer clear of them. If you have an issue with a member of the Nudds family, report the matter to the police and leave it to them.'

Nancy came in with a tray, placed it on Underwood's desk and left. He handed me a mug of tea with *Arsenal* on it in bright red letters, then offered me a custard cream.

'Previous?' I queried, declining the custard cream.

'The Nuddses come from south of the river,' Underwood said. 'They're an old criminal family – a dynasty, you might say. Christopher and Blanche's grandfather, Patrick Nudds, was hanged in 1938 for shooting a constable in Bromley High Street. Patrick's son Johnnie Nudds – that's Christopher and Blanche's dad –

moved north of the river some years ago with the rest of the family. Johnnie got himself committed to Broadmoor soon afterwards and he's still there. These days, the family business is run by his son Christopher. His friends call him Kiff.'

'Family business?'

'Drugs. Property. Stolen goods.'

'But how can I be sure that Janet Connor – the woman I knew as Janet Connor – is Blanche Nudds?' I said. 'Isn't that pure speculation? I'm going to need a positive identification—'

'It's all in the report, Mr Quirke, all in the report,' Underwood said. 'It wasn't difficult to get pictures of Kiff. He did a two-year stretch not very long ago. Look.'

He tilted the screen towards me, scrolled down, highlighted a police mugshot and enlarged it. The lean face and haircut were unmistakable. I was looking at Rick.

'He was sent down for…' Underwood scrolled again. 'Let's see … receiving stolen goods. Here it is – a Lexus sports car. Concealing it in his garage. And he got a confiscation order for £140,000, to be paid within three months.'

That sounded like Rick. 'What about Janet?' I said.

'Blanche? Photos of her were harder to find because she hasn't got a police record,' Underwood said. 'However, we did come up with this.'

Another picture appeared on the screen, grainy but clear enough for the purposes of identification. It had been taken at a charity fundraising dinner eighteen months earlier, Underwood told me. His assistant had sourced it in a back number of a glossy society magazine. I leaned forward to get a good look. Four diners, two men and two women, sat round a table in a crowded restaurant. There were so many champagne bottles, glasses and candlesticks on the table that it would have been difficult to fit anything else on. The men wore dinner jackets and black ties, the women evening dresses. Rick was easily recognisable. He was having a good time, laughing into the camera. Very much in the party mood, our Rick. I wondered if he had a gun in his pocket. The woman sitting opposite him was Janet. She was wearing a sleeveless black gown and jewellery. She looked classy. But she always did.

Underwood enlarged the picture and pointed to the names underneath. *Mr Eagon Chadwick, Ms Blanche Nudds, Mrs Sarah Chadwick, Mr Christopher Nudds…*

'OK,' I said, 'so that's who she is. Blanche Nudds. That's fine, Mr Underwood. It's all I need to know. Not Janet Connor, Blanche Nudds.'

They'd pulled off one hell of a hoax.

26

'You wanted a story,' I said to Phil when he got back from Newcastle. 'I've got one. Their name is Nudds.'

'That's a story?'

I handed him the final tracing report, an update of the interim one. Underwood had sent it by courier and it contained a startling revelation. Not only had the untiring Mr Underwood given us the Nuddses' home address in Ingatestone, he'd provided a list of their assets. These included directorships of several companies, one of which was none other than the Willoughby Art Gallery. According to its entry in the Companies House register, which Underwood had obligingly copied for us, the gallery had three directors: Blanche Nudds, with a holding of 2,268 ordinary shares, her brother Kiff, who had another 2,268 and David Platinga, the managing director, who had 4,583.

'This is dynamite,' Phil said. 'Blanche Nudds must have known Doug Hamilton. It's coming together.'

I couldn't see how. My scepticism must have shown in my face because Phil started to lecture me. 'Don't you get it?' he said. 'Doug was working for the Nuddses.'

'What? Painting pictures for their gallery?'

Phil laid a hand on my shoulder. 'Selling drugs, like you've always said. He wasn't selling them for Vilday, he was selling them for the Nuddses. He must have crossed Vilday in the process, so Vilday killed him.'

'But what has this got to do with Janet?'

'Don't you see where Blanche comes in? Really? You disappoint me. Let me explain. Doug starts dealing for Blanche and her brother Kiff. Unfortunately, he gets too enthusiastic and strays into Vilday's territory. Vilday is also dealing – that's what your psychologist friend said, isn't it? Dealers are touchy about territory. So Vilday gets rid of Doug, and the Nuddses aren't best pleased. Maybe Doug was one of their key men. Maybe they liked him, nothing more than that. Who knows? But that's where you come in. The Nuddses want to take Vilday out, but they don't want to spark a gangland vendetta. So they con you into going after Vilday on their behalf. It's not Conrad's death they want to avenge, it's Doug's. That's the scam. And Blanche pulls it off brilliantly.'

'*Almost* pulls it off,' I said.

'All right – to save your feelings, almost pulls it off. But it doesn't alter the fact that they had you for their patsy.'

'Sounds like you're working up another plot for your TV series, Phil.'

That annoyed him. 'You're in more danger than ever,' he said, reddening. 'Vilday probably thinks you're after him with your gun.'

'But I'm not.'

'He knows what you did with it in Tooth Lane. He probably thinks that he'll be next.'

'I still don't get it,' I said. 'Where does Conrad fit in? And why was Blanche pretending to be his sister?'

'You're a bit slow today,' Phil said. 'Blanche attended the trial because Doug had been selling drugs for her. When the eleven-to-one verdict came through and she realised you were the one, she decided to go to work on you. She played on your sympathy for Conrad. And you went along with it like an idiot.'

'I don't think so. It's too far-fetched.'

Phil guffawed. 'Trust me, everything fits together perfectly. You wanted to prove that Conrad was wrongfully convicted. So when Blanche told you that Doug was murdered by Vilday, you went after him. Now he's after you.'

I didn't say a thing.

'If only you hadn't been taken in by that devious woman.'

'Taken in?' I yelled. 'She wasn't acting, you bastard. She was hurting. I could tell.'

Phil must have realised he'd gone too far, because he jumped up, pulled me to my feet and gave me a bear hug. 'Aw, Tony, don't go all huffy on me.' He dragged me round the room in an ungainly, lolloping dance that nearly had us on the floor. 'It's only old Phil sounding off again,' he wailed. 'Been a long day.'

Phil's theory fitted a lot of the facts, but not all of them. Janet – I still found it difficult to think of her as Blanche – might have fooled me about her identity, but I knew she wasn't faking her grief. That was genuine, and Phil's theory didn't explain why. But I didn't want to get into another argument.

'What do we do now?' I said.

'Take a closer look at Doug's background. Find solid evidence that he was dealing for the Nuddses.'

'I've tried that,' I said. 'Conrad's father told me both boys were clean.'

'So they deceived him.'

Mr Connor was a decent, upright citizen. But he could hardly be described as streetwise. 'OK,' I said. 'How am I supposed to get this so-called solid evidence?'

'Talk to someone else who knew Doug.'

I thought of his part-time job. 'How about his former workmates,' I said, 'at the builders' yard?'

Fearings of Purfleet the blue-and-white sign said. I took a good look at the security hut as I drove through the gates. The guard glanced up from whatever he was doing, but didn't challenge me. That was where Doug must have spent his shifts. It would have been a good place to sell drugs. Anybody could walk off the street and call in there. I drove past a stack of railway sleepers and parked in the customer car park.

A lot of effort had gone into making the yard secure. The ten-foot fence round the perimeter was topped with

221

razor wire and there were arc lights every thirty yards. High-value items – brand new concrete mixers, mini-diggers and the like – were lined up inside a compound of their own. I looked everywhere for a member of staff without success. The only sign of activity was a forklift truck loading corrugated sheeting in the distance. Next to it, a single-storey building had *Sales & Enquiries* over the door. I set off walking towards it.

'Need any help?'

A skinny youth had emerged from a barn-like structure in the middle of the yard. He was carrying a plastic bucket full of chrome door handles.

'I'm looking for some timber,' I said. 'Six fence posts and five – no, fifteen – lengths like that one.' I pointed to a pile of planks on the top shelf of the barn.

'Not sure we've got fifteen.' The youth put down his bucket, disappeared behind the barn and came back with an extendable ladder. I waited at the bottom as he climbed up and counted the planks.

'Nine,' he shouted down. 'Want me to get them for you?'

'No,' I shouted back. 'If there's only nine, I'll leave it.'

He came down the ladder. 'I'll get the fence posts.'

'On second thoughts,' I said, 'I'll leave them too. Worked here long, have you?'

He wasn't sure what to make of that. 'Eighteen months,' he said after some hesitation.

'You'll have known Doug Hamilton, then.'

He didn't give me an answer, but I knew it was a yes.

'I'm a relative of his,' I said. 'His mum's quite upset. About what happened, I mean.'

'Right,' said the youth, picking up his bucket.

'Friendly with him, were you?' I said.

The youth wanted to walk off but he didn't have the nerve. 'Doug was on nights,' he said. 'Nights and weekends. I don't do nights.'

'See much of him outside work?'

The youth looked away as if I was embarrassing him.

'A lot of lads do,' I said. 'Get together with their mates after work.'

'We weren't mates,' he said, still avoiding my eyes.

'Everything all right, Gary?' The question was accompanied by the clump of wellies behind me. It came from an employee with a grey beard and pebble glasses. The *Fearings* lettering on his donkey jacket had faded almost away.

'Customer wants to know about Doug,' the youth said. He sounded glad to hand over the responsibility.

The employee in the donkey jacket looked at me cautiously. 'Doug Hamilton? What about him?'

'It's personal,' I said, and repeated the line about being a relative.

Donkey Jacket sucked his teeth, then said to the youth, 'Gary, there's an order for cap screws that needs making up.' He nodded in the direction of Sales & Enquiries. 'Take care of it for me, will you?'

Gary loped off thankfully, swinging his bucket.

'Hamilton doesn't work here any more,' Donkey Jacket said. 'I'm not sure I can tell you anything about him.'

223

'If it's a matter of expenses,' I said, 'I might be able to come to an arrangement.'

There was a short pause. 'What exactly do you want to know?'

'We've heard a lot of rumours about Doug,' I said, 'and they aren't nice ones. I want to know if they're true.'

'You from the papers?'

'I just told you. I'm a relative.'

Donkey Jacket glanced up at the nearest CCTV camera. Then he looked in the direction of Sales & Enquiries. 'How much?'

'Hundred quid?' I was prepared to go higher, but it wasn't necessary.

'OK,' he said, 'but I can't talk now.'

'When?'

'I come off at six. That any good?'

'Fine,' I said. 'Is there somewhere we can sit down?'

'The Bricklayers?'

'What's that?'

'It's a pub on the London Road,' he said, pointing to the gates. 'Left when you leave the yard, then right at the lights. I can be there by six fifteen.'

'I'll see you there,' I said. 'My name's Tony Quirke, by the way.'

'Miles.'

'See you later, Miles.'

27

I'd half-expected Miles not to turn up, but when I walked into the Bricklayers Arms he was waiting for me.

'First things first,' I said. 'What are you having?'

He said he drank bitter. I went to the bar and came back with a pint for him and a half for me.

'Cheers,' I said.

'Cheers.' He lifted his glass to his lips. 'What do you want to know?' He seemed smaller without the donkey jacket. Less sure of himself, too.

'I'm here on behalf of Doug's mother,' I said. 'There's a lot of stories going round about Doug. What he was getting up to. They've upset her and she wants to know if there's any truth in them.' I broke off as if I'd given too much away already. 'Maybe you're not the person I ought to be asking.'

'Oh yes,' Miles said quickly, 'I worked with him. Doug was security, so he wasn't on the yard. But I'm a supervisor and I saw a lot of him.'

He wanted the hundred quid.

'So, what sort of a bloke was he?'

'Doug was a good lad,' Miles said. 'Worked hard, never late. A bit quiet, but there wasn't no side to him. He was on the gates, you know. Yeah, Doug was all right.'

I got out my wallet, showed him five twenties, folded them in half and closed my fist round them. 'Does the name Nudds mean anything to you?' I said.

Miles gave me a blank look.

'Christopher Nudds? His friends call him Kiff.'

The blank look didn't alter.

'Blanche Nudds?'

Miles shifted uncomfortably. 'We might have had a customer by that name. I could look it up if you want—'

'Did Doug ever mention them?' I said. 'That's all I need to know.'

Miles shook his head and took a mouthful of beer. He had rotten teeth and didn't look as if he used much soap.

'Run your eyes over this,' I said, getting out my phone and showing him the mugshot of Kiff Nudds. 'Ever see this guy?'

Miles looked at it. 'Nope.'

'Think back,' I said, 'to when Doug was on the gates. Did you ever see anyone like this hanging around? Chatting to him, perhaps?'

'No way,' said Miles.

'OK,' I said. 'Thanks.'

Miles looked at my fist, the one holding the money.

'Now,' I said, 'the main thing I wanted to ask about was drugs. I'm going to put it to you straight, Miles, and I'd appreciate a straight answer. Doug's mum has heard a rumour that he was selling illegal drugs. As I said, it's upset her. She wants to be sure, one way or the other. Do you think there's any truth in it?'

Miles shook his head vigorously. 'Sell illegal drugs? Doug Hamilton? He wouldn't have worked at Fearings if he was dealing drugs. Do you know what we get paid? Anyway, I knew the bloke. Doug never did drugs, that's a cert. He did other things, fucking stupid things, but he never did drugs.'

I decided to take Miles at his word. What reason could he have for lying? 'I guess that clears it up,' I said. 'Mrs Hamilton will be pleased when I tell her. Thank you for putting her mind at rest.'

He looked at his glass. It was empty.

I went to the bar and bought him another. Carrying it back to our table, I wondered whether to give him his hundred and call it a day. But he seemed to know what he was talking about. So I thought I'd pump him for more.

'I wish I'd known Doug better,' I said. 'Did he ever mention his paintings?'

Miles looked mystified.

'He was an artist in his spare time,' I said. 'He even had some pictures for sale in a gallery. I was wondering if he ever mentioned them to you.'

'Never said a dicky bird about paintings.'

'Did he ever mention his flatmate?'

'What, the one who killed him?'

'Conrad Connor.'

Miles considered the question carefully, then shook his head. He was a man of few words but his meanings were clear.

'You told me Doug did some stupid things,' I said. 'What exactly did you mean?'

Miles shrugged.

'Here,' I said. 'You can have the hundred now if you tell me what stupid things.'

Miles took the money. 'You know we had a robbery a while back?' he began.

I thought of the razor wire and the arc lights and shook my head.

'Well, we did,' Miles said. 'It happened one Sunday when Doug was on the gates. We was closed, of course, but this guy drives up in a van and says he's come to collect some ridge tiles that got left behind. So Doug lets him in, the muppet. Once the van's inside, another geezer jumps out the back. The two of them take Doug's walkie-talkie off of him, tie him up, stick him in the garden supplies shed and pile fencing against the door so he can't get out. Then they set about pinching stuff.'

'How can you blame Doug for that?' I said. 'What's stupid about getting jumped by robbers and locked in a shed?'

'He should never have opened the gates, that's what was stupid,' Miles said. 'Not when we was closed. It's a strict rule. He should have known. He was security, wasn't he?'

'What happened to him?' I said.

'I can tell you what should have happened. He should have got the sack.'

'You think so?'

Miles nodded. 'Of course. But he didn't. I reckon Doug had friends up top. Anyone else would have been through the gates so fast their feet wouldn't have touched the floor.' He smoothed the twenties between work-stained fingers, folded them carefully and put them in his back pocket.

'Did the robbers get away with much?' I said.

'Nah, the police caught them in the act. Even so, Doug should have got the sack. Bet he felt a fool when they let him out of that shed.'

'I suppose it was a bit stupid,' I said.

Miles sniggered.

Opening the gates to a gang of robbers, I said to myself. What else would you expect from an artist?

Miles emptied his glass, wiped his mouth with the back of his hand and stood up. 'Anything else you want to know? The missus'll be wondering where I am.'

'No, you've been very helpful,' I said.

We made our way to the exit.

'And you're absolutely sure Doug wasn't doing drugs?' I said as we left the pub.

'It's a load of bollocks,' Miles said. 'If I'd thought as much, I'd have reported him. You can tell that to his mother. I'll tell her myself, if it would help.'

He couldn't have made it clearer. 'Want a lift?' I said.

'No thanks, I'll walk.' Miles stuffed his hands in his pockets and was halfway across the car park when he stopped dead. It looked as if he'd forgotten something.

'Funny thing was,' he said, turning to face me, 'the police was waiting for them.'

'Waiting for who? The robbers? I'm afraid I don't get you, Miles.'

'There's people,' he said, 'say they saw police vans parked up Priory Lane that Sunday morning. Two vanloads of coppers at nine thirty, tucked away round the back of Fearings.' Miles screwed up his face as if he was struggling to get to the bottom of it. 'The robbers didn't turn up till a quarter to eleven.' He stood there looking puzzled for a moment, then continued on his way.

'You've lost me,' I called after him. 'Where's Priory Lane?'

He didn't reply and was soon out of earshot, walking briskly along the main road. Within minutes he'd disappeared among the crowds of commuters returning home from work.

'You're barking up the wrong tree,' I said to Phil when I got back to Putney. 'According to Doug's workmates, he wasn't dealing. Mr Connor was right all along.'

I don't think anything would have shaken Phil out of his obsession that Doug was selling drugs for the Nuddses. 'We'll have to keep digging away until we find evidence that proves it,' he said. 'All these little stories have got to fit together somehow.'

'There's too many little stories. Too much detail.'

'The devil is in the detail,' Phil said. 'Speaking of the devil, why don't you go back to the shrink who put the finger on Vilday in the first place? He seemed to know a lot about the Riverwell drug scene.'

'Go back to Brayne-Thompson?' I said. 'I did think of it—'

'He's the one who started the whole thing off, isn't he? He's the one who got in touch with Janet—' Phil broke off, looking perplexed. 'But she wasn't Janet, was she? Hold on – how come he didn't realise that? You said he knew her family, didn't you?'

'He'd been treating a relative of hers. Or so she said.'

'And he'd phoned her.'

I thought back. 'That's right, he'd phoned her. Said there was something she needed to know.'

'So he must have known who she was,' Phil said. 'That's very odd. You ought to talk to him and clear it up.'

Phil certainly had a point. But I raised my hands in protest. 'I haven't got a lot of holiday left.'

'One last throw of the dice.'

'Tell you what,' I said. 'Let's get Underwood to run a background check on him first.'

Phil agreed that this would be a good idea. So I sent Underwood an email requesting an in-depth investigation of Kenneth Brayne-Thompson, psychotherapist. I asked for social media searches, a financial status report, his employment history, a criminal records search, property ownership and possible aliases. The lot. And Phil promised to pay for it.

'Now,' he said, 'fancy a bourbon? I brought a cracker back from the States. You'll like this one. Barrel strength, sixty-three per cent. Like pouring distilled rattlesnake down your throat.'

Phil had left for work when I got up the following morning. I pulled on my overcoat and went for a walk along the Putney embankment to clear my head. The cold air was good for that. The view was good for nothing. Slimy pebbles lay exposed by the low tide as far as the eye could see. The sky was the colour of lead. A couple of hundred yards upstream from Putney Bridge I passed a small boat moored offshore. Its owner, the only living soul in sight, was pulling a cover over his pride and joy. The rest of the population had been sensible enough to stay indoors.

I was beginning to wonder where we were going with the book project. There was little that made sense now – no theme, no logic, no underpinning narrative. All the snippets of information people had given me, so promising at the time, seemed as meaningful as the brown froth blowing disconsolately along the shoreline. For want of something better to do, I got out my phone, turned my back to the wind and looked up the Vilday rape case on the internet.

All I found was a mention in an evening newspaper.

RAPE TRIAL COLLAPSES
The trial of a man accused of rape has ended in

acquittal after the alleged victim withdrew her evidence. The accused, Gregory Emmanuel Vilday, met the alleged victim in a West End nightclub. The trial collapsed in January and on Monday the Crown Prosecution Service said there was no reasonable prospect of a conviction. The accused was found not guilty and acquitted by Judge Margaret Smithers at a brief hearing at Wood Green Crown Court earlier today.

I thought back to my visit to Colin Christie. How could a young woman be taken in by a man like Vilday? What sort of threats had made her withdraw her testimony? Why had she believed that jumping in front of a train was her only option when she heard that Vilday had escaped justice? I would never know the answers. I would never even know her name.

Or would I?

I leaned on the embankment railings and stared into the muddy water. There was a date on the newspaper article I'd just read. The article said that the case against Vilday had been dismissed earlier that day. And Colin had told me that the victim had jumped in front of a train as soon as she heard.

I typed 'tube train death Clapham North' into my browser, added the date of Vilday's Crown Court hearing, then hit search.

WOMAN JUMPS TO DEATH IN TUBE
Horrified onlookers saw an 18-year-old secretary

jump in front of a Tube train at Clapham North station. Flora Nudds was taken to St Georges Hospital...

Nudds? That was a name you didn't come across every day.

28

The drives were full of BMWs, Mercs and Lexuses and the garages were doubles. I drove slowly past the Nudds residence in Ingatestone, parked fifty yards down the road and walked back. Unlike their neighbours' front gardens, which were laid out with ponds, ornamental trees and miniature hedges, the frontage of the Nudds property was a bleak expanse of asphalt. Its only concession to the middle-class pretensions of the neighbourhood was the Bentley parked outside the massive bay window.

I had to confront Blanche face-to-face. Not only did I have a burning desire to tell her she'd been found out, it was the only way I could know for sure whether Doug had been dealing for her. And I had questions to ask about Flora Nudds. Feeling a rush of adrenalin, I walked up to the red-painted front door and pressed the shiny brass bell.

The woman who'd told me bigger lies than anyone I'd ever known looked the same as when I'd last seen her. It was only the astonishment on her face that was different.

'Hello, Janet,' I said. I didn't want to reveal my hand too soon.

She swallowed.

'Can I come in?'

'Come in?' she said. 'You've got a bloody nerve,' and tried to slam the door on me.

I shoved it back in her face. They either jump out of the way or they're knocked out of the way, in either case you're in. Blanche retreated several yards down the hall.

'What do you want, turning up like this?'

I shut the door behind me. 'Is Rick in?'

She looked at me as if I'd spat on her mother's grave. 'He's still in custody, you bastard.'

That suited me fine. I glanced round the hall. It was spacious, almost grand, with white-painted doors leading off. A red-carpeted staircase ascended to the first floor. Blanche continued to back away, finally taking up a position on the bottom stair.

'I'm not going to hurt you,' I said. 'I'm after information, that's all.'

She waited for me to make my move. As appealing as she looked in her designer jeans and pale blue fluffy cardigan, I remembered what she'd been prepared to do to me.

'I only want to talk,' I said.

She came down from the stair. Thrusting her hands

in the pockets of her jeans, she looked me up and down. 'You don't have to tell me what happened,' she said. 'You ratted on us.'

I shrugged.

'Rick said you were shitting yourself in the car. We should have got someone with balls.'

'Can we sit down and talk?' I said.

'Better come in here.' Opening one of the doors, she let me into a massive sitting room. It had wall-to-wall carpeting, a marble fireplace, a scattering of Persian rugs and expensive-looking furniture. In the far corner, one of the biggest TVs I've ever seen stared blankly back at me. And through the bay window I could see the Bentley on the forecourt. Nice.

'This is about Doug Hamilton,' I said when we'd seated ourselves. Blanche had taken the sofa next to the fireplace. I'd chosen an armchair with my back to the bay window. It put the light behind me, which always helps with a difficult conversation. 'Doug's someone I know nothing about,' I said.

'I thought you were supposed to be good at finding things out,' was the reply. She was mocking me. 'Fat lot of good you turned out to be.'

'Look,' I said, 'I'm sorry about Rick. But you can't blame me for what happened.'

There was derision in her eyes. 'You know what you are? Pathetic.'

I wondered how long we could keep up the pretence, both of us. I decided to jump straight in.

'You knew Doug quite well, didn't you?' I said.

She stiffened. 'What makes you think I knew Doug Hamilton?'

'The Willoughby Art Gallery.'

She almost fell off the sofa. 'What do you know about the Willoughby?'

'You own it.'

'I don't own it.'

'Come off it, you've got 2,268 shares. And that's not all. Doug was working for you, wasn't he? But he wasn't painting pretty pictures. What was he doing, Blanche?'

She gasped at the mention of her name. She must have wondered what else I knew.

'Because that's who you are,' I said. 'Blanche Nudds. Why were you pretending to be Janet Connor?'

She looked out of the window as if she was expecting someone. I needed to hurry things along.

'If you're not Conrad's sister,' I said, 'you must have been at the trial because of Doug. You went there every day. You told me. And I saw you.'

'Of course I knew Doug,' she said. 'He was a nice lad. He didn't deserve to die. I went to the trial to see Connor get what was coming to him. Conrad bloody Connor – what a leech. Hanging round the gallery hoping we'd take him on, would you believe? Just because we were showing some of his flatmate's paintings. The day Connor hanged himself I laughed myself silly.'

The brutality of her words shocked me. This was the real Janet. The woman who'd revealed her colours in the Aveley House flat, if not her name. 'But why did you pretend?' I said. 'Why did you want me to think you were Janet Connor?'

238

No reply.

'You wanted Vilday dead, of course you did,' I said. 'But it was nothing to do with Conrad Connor, was it? You wanted Vilday dead because of what he did to Flora.'

Blanche couldn't have looked more stunned if I'd slapped her in the face.

'Who was Flora?'

She didn't answer.

'I believed you,' I said. 'I didn't think anyone could fake grief like that. But you weren't grieving about Conrad, were you? You were grieving about Flora. Who was she, Blanche?'

She stared at me, then licked her lips. 'Have you ever had to identify a dead body?'

I shook my head.

'Your own flesh and blood? Someone you grew up with? No, you haven't. So how do you think it affected me? Flora was eighteen, Tony, eighteen. My little sister and my best friend in all the world. I never stop thinking about her.'

'It sickened me when I heard,' I said.

She looked out of the window again.

'You had me fooled,' I said. 'You thought you could wrap me round your little finger.'

Recovering herself a little, she said, 'I did, though, didn't I?'

It was a remark which I decided to ignore. 'I'm sorry about Flora,' I said. 'Vilday ought to pay for what he did to her, nobody's arguing about that. He's the lowest of the low. Can't you see we're on the same side?'

She didn't look as if she did.

'I've been nosing round Fearings,' I said. 'Where Doug was a security guard. He worked there because he was hard up, then all of a sudden he came into a large sum of money. Where did it come from? It wasn't from selling paintings, was it? He hadn't sold a single one.'

Blanche kept her lips firmly shut.

'I know about your family,' I said. 'I know about the drugs and the stolen goods. I think Doug was working for you and your brother. Selling drugs for you. I think he had a run-in with Vilday, maybe strayed into his territory, and that's why Vilday got rid of him. All I want from you is information that'll connect Vilday to Doug's murder. You must know something. Tell me and I'll go away.'

She still didn't say anything.

'What did Vilday have against Doug?' I said. 'Why won't you tell me why he killed him?'

She gave me a withering look. 'Because Vilday didn't kill him.'

Not for the first time since I met Blanche Nudds I experienced a sense of detachment from reality. Without any conviction in my voice, I heard myself say, 'Come on, Blanche, you can't mean that.'

She tossed her head. 'Of course I mean it. Doug Hamilton was killed by Conrad Connor. Who else?'

Christ, I thought. If it was true, if Conrad was the murderer, it would make me the biggest fool—

A puzzled look was spreading over Blanche's face. She must have wondered why her words were having such an effect. She understood soon enough, because the puzzlement was replaced by a grin of triumph. And it was that grin – more of a smirk, in fact – that jogged me out of my moment of self-doubt.

'Nice try,' I said, 'but there's something you've forgotten, Blanche. Our meeting with Brayne-Thompson. You've forgotten what he told us about Vilday. Remember? "That was my gun"? "I'd had all I could stand from Hamilton"?'

It only seemed to amuse her.

'It looks like I'll have to hurt you,' I said, bringing out the PK-32. It was still packing four rounds. 'Neat little helper, don't you think?' I aimed it between her eyes. 'Tell me what happened, Blanche. You know you don't have a choice.'

The look of amusement vanished and a shiver ran through her body.

'Why did Greg Vilday kill Doug Hamilton?'

'Don't,' she said, her eyes on the gun.

That wasn't what I wanted to hear. 'I will count to five,' I said. 'Then I'll pull the trigger. One.'

No reply.

'You'll have to tell me sooner or later, Blanche. Two.'

Still no reply.

'Three.'

'Vilday didn't do it,' she said. 'He had no reason to.' She was shaking so badly she could hardly get the words out.

'I don't think you're being completely frank with me. Four.'

The next sounds that passed her lips were whimpers.

'This is your last chance,' I said.

She started to mumble something. I leaned forward to catch her words but they were lost in the roar of a motorbike. It drove into the forecourt and coughed itself into silence outside the bay window.

Blanche looked out. Twisting my head round, I saw a man in leathers straddling a gleaming Royal Enfield. He leaned back in the seat, took off his helmet and hung it on the handlebars. He was young, with curly blond hair and a yellow scarf round his neck. Swinging one leg off the bike, he pushed down the kickstand and clumped towards the front door in his motorcycle boots. I couldn't tear my eyes away.

That was my mistake. Because the time I spent looking out of the window gave Blanche her chance. She jumped off the sofa, grabbed the barrel of the PK-32 and tried to twist it out of my hand. I soon got it back but fumbled and dropped it. I was trying to keep my finger off the trigger. It only took seconds to pick up again, but by then Blanche was halfway to the door.

I would never have shot her, no matter what, so all I could do was watch her disappear. I looked out of the window again. The blond biker was nowhere to be seen. Then I heard Blanche talking to him in the hall. I couldn't hear what they were saying, but I didn't need to. I covered the half-open sitting room door with the PK-32, expecting him to burst in at any moment.

Instead, the door slammed shut and someone turned a key in the lock. All without a word being said. I lowered the gun. Shit.

At first, my plan was to smash a window pane and get out of the house that way. Unfortunately, I soon discovered that the bay window was double-glazed. I went to the door and listened. Silence. I thought about the window again. A closer inspection revealed that it was lockable. Somewhere there must be a key. People usually keep them on the mantelpiece, so that was where I looked. I didn't find one, not even in the pretty Wedgware jugs on either side of the black marble clock.

'Blanche!' I shouted, banging on the door. 'Blanche! Open up!'

Silence.

Pressing the muzzle of the PK-32 against the lock, I pulled the trigger. There was a mighty crash and a cloud of smoke. When it cleared, I found that I'd destroyed a lot of wood but that was all. The lock had held. But at least I could see what was needed. Two more shots in quick succession blew out the strike plate and the door swung free. I kicked it open and stood well back, gun at the ready.

I had one round left. Chambered and ready to go.

My only desire was to get out of the house. The hall was deserted, so I ran for the front door.

Bam! A bullet buried itself in the wall next to my head, showering me with plaster. Swinging round, I saw the blond biker halfway up the stairs, framed against the big window at the top. He was pointing a handgun at me. The idea of a gun fight in Blanche's house didn't make sense, but I was trapped. It would be suicide to continue to the front door, so I ran back the way I'd come.

Bam! This time the bullet missed me by a mile.

Once back in the sitting room, I took cover inside the doorway. From there I was able to peer round the door post and level the PK-32.

Whack! The shot I got off was well-aimed. The blond boy must have fired at the same time, although I didn't hear the shot. I only knew he'd fired because the door trim above my head exploded into a cloud of splinters.

There was no hiding place, but I went looking for one. That's how desperate I was. I ended up in the far corner of the room, crouching behind an armchair. I was kidding myself that the blond boy wouldn't be able to see me when he came looking. How stupid was that? But my gun was empty. When you're defenceless you'll try anything.

Seconds passed like hours. All I could hear was the whine of a leaf blower further down the road. Why hadn't the blond boy shown himself? I looked at the PK-32 in my hand. It was greasy with sweat but there was no chance of it slipping out of my grasp. The pattern on the grip was doing its job. The genius who designed it must have known how a shooter's body reacts when his life is on the line. He sweats gallons.

'Hey!' I shouted, hoping to negotiate a way out.

No reply.

'Hey!'

Still nothing.

The leaf blower stopped blowing.

I don't know how long I crouched there. It was probably no more than a minute. Everything had gone quiet, so I made my way slowly forward. I stood to the left of the door, the position from which I'd fired my shot. I was still holding the PK-32 at the ready. If the blond boy saw it, he'd think it was loaded.

It was then that I noticed the ejected cartridge cases. Four of them. They lay on the carpet at my feet, surrounded by splinters of wood and pieces of plaster. Would I never learn? I picked them up, put them in my pocket, counted to ten and chanced a quick look.

The blond boy, whoever he might have been, was sitting halfway up the stairs with his head in his hands, dripping blood. His gun lay on the next stair down. I couldn't tell how badly he was hurt, but the way out was clear.

I sprinted the fifty yards to my Volvo faster than I'd run anywhere in my life. Things had got out of hand, but I couldn't be blamed for that. I started the engine, looked behind me in the mirror and my anxiety began to subside. There was no traffic, no pedestrians, not even a man with a leaf blower. I spent a few moments picking splinters of wood out of my scalp, then pulled away from the kerb and jammed the accelerator to the floor. After a hundred yards, the road curved to the left and I slowed to a comfortable thirty. My phone pinged but I left it in my pocket. Although the road ahead was clear, there might be a patrol car lurking up a side road. I didn't want to be caught breaking the law.

To cover my tracks, I drove for several miles before parking in a quiet cul-de-sac. It was only there that I got out my phone and looked at the email I'd received. It was from Underwood.

Dear Mr Quirke,
CUSTOMER CONTRACT REFERENCE NO:
C001502 – ENHANCED TRACING REPORT
Re: Brayne-Thompson, Kenneth
EMPLOYMENT
Kenneth Brayne-Thompson was struck off the
register of the Health and Care Professions Council
two years ago. He now practises as an unregistered
psychotherapist in North London.
CRIMINAL RECORD
In addition to running his legitimate practice,
Brayne-Thompson established a bogus psychotherapy
clinic, the sole purpose of which was to submit fake
VAT repayment claims to the tax authorities. He
also falsified invoices and bank statements. He was
convicted of the VAT offence and given a two-year
prison sentence suspended for 18 months.
FAMILY
Kenneth Brayne-Thompson's parents were Joseph
Thompson, described in the census as a domestic
gardener, and Martha Jane Nudds, a school teacher.
He was born—

I stopped reading and emailed Underwood. *Please trace
the family history of Martha Jane Nudds.*

The reply pinged into my phone as I was drawing
up outside Phil's flat. That was some email. It turned
everything I knew about the murder on its head.

29

'No,' I insisted. 'Don't you see? We're going to need a whole new storyline.'

We were sitting in Holly's office in tree-lined Queen's Road, Wimbledon. Her one-woman literary agency occupied the top floor of a tall Victorian house, an imposing edifice with iron railings out front and well-worn marble steps up to the door.

Holly, a slim and stylishly dressed woman in her forties, was giving me a disapproving frown. I was trying to explain to her and Phil that we'd been following a false trail. To me, it was obvious. But they were proving hard to convince.

'I'll go through it again,' I said. 'After the trial, a woman comes up to me and tells me that she's Conrad's sister Janet. She begs me to clear his name. I go along with it and start punching holes in the prosecution case. But she insists that we need to do more than that. She wants me to discover who really did kill Doug. There'll always be room for doubt about Conrad's innocence until we prove that the murderer was someone else.'

'Agreed,' said Holly.

'So I start to look for the killer. Very conveniently, Janet turns up with someone called Kenneth Brayne-Thompson, a psychotherapist in private practice. Brayne-Thompson informs me that Doug was killed by a client of his called Greg Vilday. Everything he says about Vilday checks out – the way he looks, the jewellery he wears, the violent past. So I start investigating Vilday and get beaten up for my pains. Thus far, everything makes sense. Until I learn that Janet Connor is dead and the woman I've been dealing with is called Blanche Nudds.

'I already know that Vilday committed rape and got away with it. Now it turns out that his victim was Blanche's sister Flora, an eighteen-year-old secretary. Tragically, Flora took her own life when she learned that Vilday had escaped justice. That's the real reason Blanche is after him. That's why she wants revenge. She isn't after Vilday for the Doug Hamilton murder. She even tells me that he didn't do it.

'At first, I don't believe her. I'm certain that Vilday killed Doug because of what Brayne-Thompson told us in the Brookmyre Hotel. He was very convincing. Who's right? I ask myself. Blanche or Brayne-Thompson? There's only one way to find out – put Underwood on to Brayne-Thompson.'

I got out my phone and showed Holly Underwood's last email. 'Our ever-efficient skip tracer investigates

Brayne-Thompson's family background,' I said. 'He discovers that his mother, a woman called Martha Nudds, has a brother called Johnnie Nudds. Johnnie is a hard case, currently resident in Broadmoor. So what? you might ask. Here's what – Johnnie Nudds happens to be Blanche's father. Which means that Blanche and Brayne-Thompson are cousins.'

I paused, confident that they would see the light. But Holly's face was still full of doubt. She handed the phone back with a dismissive flick of her wrist. That wasn't the way I'd been hoping she'd take it.

'Blanche made out that she didn't know Brayne-Thompson,' I said. 'But he was her cousin. Come off it! They were in it together. The meeting at the Brookmyre was a set-up. It was intended to send me after Vilday.

'According to Underwood, Brayne-Thompson is a con man. I can only conclude that what he told me about Vilday – the midnight phone calls, the confession, how he was supplying Doug with drugs – was a pack of lies. And because Brayne-Thompson's word is the only evidence we've got that Vilday killed Doug Hamilton, we're back where we started.'

Holly still wasn't having it.

'Just hear me out,' I said. 'Blanche attended the trial because she knew Doug Hamilton through the art gallery. She believed he'd been killed by his flatmate, and she went along to see Conrad get his comeuppance. When the verdict was announced, she saw how I reacted and guessed I was the juror who wanted to let him off.'

'The one of the eleven-to-one,' Phil chipped in.

'Exactly,' I said. 'Blanche must have dreamed up the scam in a flash. She ran after me in the street, made out she was Conrad's sister and told me she knew he was innocent. I told her how angry I was about the way my fellow jurors had rushed to judgement. After that, she led me by the nose.'

Holly was looking at me as if I'd driven my Volvo over her pet cat. 'Why did she want *you* to go after Vilday?' she demanded. 'Why didn't she go after Vilday herself?'

'So no one could trace it to her,' I said.

Phil was shaking his head. 'I'm still convinced that Vilday killed Doug Hamilton. He's the perfect villain. The book we're writing doesn't make sense without a Vilday.'

Holly backed him up immediately. 'I've persuaded Echo Press that we've got a winner,' she said. 'If I have to go to Brenda and tell her what you're telling me, the deal will be off. No one wants to read a true crime story that ends with a question mark. But we don't have to do that. We couldn't have a better candidate for the killer than Mr Vilday. From what Phil's been telling me, he's every inch a murderer. You've done very well so far, Tony. Why give up now? Why don't you go ahead and winkle out the evidence that'll put him in the dock? We can release your book the moment he's convicted.'

I wasn't getting anywhere. That was probably because Holly didn't know the half of it. Phil hadn't told her about the gun, or what Blanche had wanted me to do with it. He hadn't told her about Tooth Lane, or the shoot-out at Blanche's. She might have seen it my way if she'd known these things, but I didn't want them getting into circulation. The police were still looking for the man who killed Brian Loughty.

'You've been through a lot recently,' said Phil. 'If you took a couple of days out—'

'There's still a book in it,' I said. 'There's a lot I want to say about the jury system. We could fill it with material about notorious miscarriages of justice. The Sally Clark case, the Stefan Kiszco case—'

'Hold on,' Holly interrupted. 'Would Vilday send men to beat you up if he wasn't guilty? He must have had a good reason for wanting to silence you.'

It was a sound point, and I didn't have an answer. I looked at Phil, hoping he would help me out. He didn't. *Think of the money,* he mouthed. Of course I was thinking of the money. But I also had to be realistic.

'Sorry, guys,' I said. 'I can't give you Greg Vilday, murderer of Douglas Hamilton, I simply can't.'

30

After Phil left for his New York convention on video games – he'd been so angry at the collapse of the book project he didn't even say goodbye – I got out the Kofler PK-32. I'd begun to think of it as a friend. But the magazine was empty. All it could do now was connect me with Tooth Lane.

I found a bottle of household bleach, a roll of cling film and a pair of rubber gloves in the kitchen. There was cotton wool in the bathroom cabinet. Pulling on the rubber gloves, I cleaned my fingerprints and DNA off the gun and cartridge cases. Then I wrapped them in the cling film. Borrowing a brown envelope and sticky tape from Phil's bureau, I made them into a neat little parcel that didn't betray its contents.

It was mid-morning. A cold wind was blowing up the Thames as I turned off the high street on to the Putney embankment. I followed it in a westerly direction, looking for a suitable resting place for the Kofler. A cabin cruiser overtook me, leaving an ever-widening V behind it. The helmsman shot a glance in my direction as he went past, reminding me how visible I was.

After a while I came to a slipway. Several cars were parked nearby, but their owners were nowhere to be seen. If I went down to the water's edge, I'd be out of range of any CCTV and doorbell cameras in the vicinity. But when I got there, close enough to smell the sour stench of the river, I noticed an old man in a grey overcoat standing at the railings a little further along. He was staring at the other side of the river, lost in thought. I didn't think he'd registered my presence, but I couldn't risk making a sudden movement, like throwing a parcel into the water.

I went back up the slipway and continued along the embankment. Soon I came to a row of four or five small boats moored several yards offshore. I stood there pretending to admire the view, the gun a dead weight in my pocket. By now, the cabin cruiser was a dot in the distance. I looked behind me. There was a little park full of young trees on the other side of the road. It was deserted. I couldn't see the houses beyond, so their cameras couldn't see me. I looked downriver towards Putney Bridge. The old man in the grey overcoat had disappeared and the embankment was clear. Upriver, I could see a figure in the distance, a jogger in red shorts and a white top. He was coming my way, but I decided to chance it. The longer I delayed, the greater the risk.

The gun went so far out I didn't even see the splash.

Not only have I wasted my annual leave, I said to myself as I walked back to Putney Bridge, not only have I lost the book deal but I've ruined the rest of my life. I've got rid of the gun, but dozens of police officers will be working on the Tooth Lane case by now. Exploring every possibility, collating evidence, drawing up psychological profiles. And if they don't come for me now, I'll have to live with the knowledge that the file will never be closed. With any luck it might be put on hold after a few months. But every two years there'll have to be a cold case review—

Turning right on to the high street, I went into one of the pubs Phil had introduced me to. The lunchtime rush hadn't started, and that suited me fine. I wasn't in a sociable mood. As the barman pulled my pint and poured me a chaser, I began to find the music irritating. It was a dreary, repetitive sixties medley. I asked the barman to turn it off. He turned it down. So I took a seat close to the door. It was draughty, but the traffic noise drowned out the music. Sinking the scotch in one, I sipped my beer and looked out on the busy high street.

Was Conrad guilty after all? The thought that he had murdered his flatmate gnawed away at me until I found myself beginning to believe it. How could I have been so stupid? The evidence on which my fellow jurors had convicted him was weak, but so was the evidence I'd gathered in his defence. Why had I taken for granted that I was right and the other eleven members of the jury were wrong?

You can't understand what a wrongful conviction does to someone unless you've seen it yourself. After he came out of prison, Dad spent every day slumped in his armchair, a glass in one hand and a bottle of whisky on the floor beside him. If you spoke to him, you'd be lucky to get a reply. If you looked into his eyes, there was nothing there. His soul had died and his body followed two years later. I'd been quick to accuse the plumber of an ulterior motive for wanting a quick conviction, but I'd had motives of my own for wanting an acquittal.

Who did you see in front of you that morning, Doug, when you found yourself looking down the barrel of a gun? Was it your flatmate Conrad Connor? Or was it a complete stranger? Did he shoot you straight away, or was there an argument? You were young and on the threshold of a promising career. That last terrible moment – did it come as a surprise, or had you been expecting it? And why would anyone want to kill you? There didn't seem to be a way of getting answers.

I bought myself another pint and sank it fast. In a corner of the pub I'd noticed a shelf packed with board games and paperbacks. I needed something to take my mind off the train wreck I'd made of my holiday, so I wandered across, conscious that the barman was watching me. There wasn't much. On the top of the pile I found a couple of kiddies' jigsaw puzzles. One was a picture of dinosaurs. The other showed Superwoman escaping from the planet Krypton as it exploded. I hadn't done a jigsaw since primary school, and I couldn't stand them even then. I put them aside, selected a fat paperback and took it to my seat. After skimming the blurb, I turned to the first chapter and started reading. But by the time

I'd reached the second page I couldn't remember what it was about. Was it a thriller or a love story? I looked at the cover again. *Famous Unsolved Murders of the Twentieth Century*.

I couldn't go on like this. I put the book back and told myself I needed something positive to focus on. Maybe it was time to leave Williams Wells and sell my skills to another company. Should I move to a different sector? Security? Credit control? I began googling job opportunities. But when I looked at my phone, all I saw was Doug's blood-soaked body on the floor of his flat.

Was there an angle on the murder that was escaping me? Information I'd acquired but hadn't taken in? Were there connections I had missed? If so, they remained frustratingly out of reach.

'I'm not sure I should serve you, sir,' the barman said when I went up to get another pint. 'Not driving today, are we?'

'Give me a fucking pint, and make the chaser a double.'

It was only when I was carrying my drinks back to my seat that it happened. The trillion-to-one chance. Somewhere in my brain, a neuron had fired and triggered a whole galaxy of other neurons. And those neurons had triggered galaxies of their own, flooding every corner of my mind with all-revealing light. If I hadn't had a glass in each hand, I would have danced a jig round the pub. I could see exactly where I'd been going wrong.

I'd been assuming I had to fit all the pieces of evidence into one big picture. But they didn't make one big picture. They made two – because there were two puzzles to be solved. The dinosaurs and Superwoman. Two jigsaw puzzles had been emptied out of their boxes on to a table and the pieces had got mixed up.

Take out the pieces representing Vilday, Blanche, Flora and Brayne-Thompson – I'd already explained to Holly and Phil what they'd been up to. That left Brian Loughty, the Drurys, Doug Hamilton and Fearings Buildings Supplies Limited.

I went to the Fearings website first. It didn't tell me anything I didn't know. But when I googled 'Fearings robbery' I got several hits. Among them, crucially, was this:

POLICE FOIL ARMED ROBBERY AT BUILDERS' YARD

Robbers brandishing shotguns threatened and bound an employee before attempting to steal products from a builders' merchants in Willeford Road, Purfleet.

The robbery took place at Fearings Buildings Supplies Limited. Two men were arrested at the scene. James Garnish (18) of Fernby Road, Laindon, and Jason Drury (20)…

31

Traffic on the South Circular was moving freely all the way to Blackheath. The approach to the Dartford Tunnel was congested, but north of the river the roads were clear again. I was way over the limit but I drove fast, ignoring speed cameras all the way, my skin clammy with sweat. Poor Doug – you must have been too surprised to shout for help, mustn't you? Surprised, because the person who came to kill you that morning was the last person you would have imagined.

Johnson Terrace looked different, although it couldn't have changed in the short time I'd been away. The same mums were pushing the same kiddies to story-time at the library. The same second-hand cars lined the kerb. It just seemed more run down. I parked in my usual spot and realised that Ma must have found a tenant for number

14. There were curtains in the front window and the *To Let* board had come down.

Hurrying across the road, I followed the alley to Drury Properties. The sign on the door said *Open*, so I went straight in. The door chime brought Ma out from the back. She looked at me in surprise, coffee mug in hand.

'Oh,' she said.

That was all. *Oh*. But she packed a lot of meaning into that one word. I wasn't welcome.

'Does the name Brian Loughty mean anything to you?' I said.

Ma flinched as if I'd stuck the PK-32 in her face. And from that moment I knew I'd got her.

'Brian Loughty,' I repeated. 'The hatchet man you sent to number 12 to beat me up. You know him, don't you? Bloody good job he did, too. The doctors said I was lucky not to lose a kidney. I wouldn't have fancied spending the rest of my life with only one kidney.'

Ma was shaking her head.

'He didn't do so well in Tooth Lane,' I said. 'When they found his body on the cobbles instead of mine, you must have been quite disappointed.'

'I don't know what you're talking about,' Ma said.

'Yes you do, Mrs Drury. You sent Brian Loughty to Tooth Lane to kill me.'

She didn't have to admit it. The look on her face told me all I needed to know. She was so shaken that coffee was slopping on the floor.

'Conrad Connor didn't kill Doug Hamilton,' I said, 'and I've made no secret of the fact that I've been looking for the man who did. I think you can tell me who that was.'

'I don't know anybody called Brian Loughty,' Ma said. 'If that's who you think killed Mr Hamilton.'

'Oh come, Mrs Drury. You must have known Brian. He was your husband's best friend. Remember when Arthur had a go at that warder in Belmarsh? Brian helped him, didn't he? They were sharing a cell. As a matter of fact, I think that Mr Loughty and your husband were even closer. Mad Brian was almost a member of your family.'

'This means nothing to me, nothing.'

'What a poor memory you have,' I said. 'Not that I blame you. You've had a lot to forget, haven't you?'

Ma slammed her mug on the desk. More coffee spilled. But it freed her right hand to jab a finger at me. 'Who do you think you are, coming in here and threatening me? Get out! Get out this instant or I'll call the police.'

'Oh no you won't,' I said. 'Not the police. You won't because I know why you got Brian Loughty to kill Doug Hamilton for you.'

Ma's eyes darted round the room, as if she was searching for something. 'I don't have to listen to this,' she said.

'It wasn't very nice of you, setting Conrad up as the killer,' I said. 'Planting the cartridges. Burying the gun where a five-year-old on an Easter egg hunt could find it. What did Conrad Connor ever do to you?'

She didn't answer me.

'Just a minute,' I said. 'We could do with a little

privacy.' I went to the front door, snapped the catch down and changed the *Open* sign to *Closed*.

'Let me tell you what happened,' I said. 'It started with the robbery at Fearings, didn't it? The one Jason went to prison for.'

'Get out of here!' Ma shouted and ran into the back room. She was making for the rear exit, I thought, so I went after her.

The back room didn't have an exit, not even a window to climb out of. It was not much more than a cupboard, with a row of grey metal filing cabinets along the back wall and a sink in the corner. Ma was standing on tiptoe, searching inside the top drawer of one of the cabinets. She didn't look like someone who'd stoop to murder, not this obliging landlady who always seemed so concerned about her tenants' welfare. But she'd found what she was looking for, and it wasn't the mobile phone I'd been expecting. It was a handgun. A semi-automatic, like my PK-32 but bigger.

Turning to face me, she pointed the gun at my chest. There was a good six feet between us. All I could do was back away. I didn't feel like trying to get it off her.

'Can you imagine the hell that Jason's going through?' she said.

I looked at the gun. 'I wouldn't use that if I were you,' I said. 'I've told someone I was coming to see you, and I've told them the reason.' It was a lie, but she couldn't have known that.

'Have you any idea,' she said, her voice shrilling, 'what it's like in prison?'

'No, I haven't,' I said. 'But Jason's prison sentence was nothing to do with me.'

'It was everything to do with Doug Hamilton,' she said.

Her finger was on the trigger. Kiff had taught me to keep my finger flat against the guard, so the gun wouldn't go off accidentally. It didn't take much pressure to fire the PK-32. I didn't know the trigger pressure of Ma's gun, but I nearly soiled my trousers thinking about it.

'Doug Hamilton put my son in prison,' she said. 'I hope he rots in hell.'

'That's why you sent Loughty to kill him, isn't it?' I said. 'Because Doug tipped off the police about the robbery. It was so easy to get Loughty to pay him back. All you had to do was open the door of the flat for him after you saw Conrad leaving for Colchester.'

'Jason was never strong,' Ma said. 'They're squeezing the life out of him. Stamping on him. Squashing him. I can't stand it. I can't go on.'

At that range she could hardly miss.

'But how did Doug know there was going to be a robbery?' I said.

Ma's eyes sank to the floor. For a moment I thought she was going to put the gun down. But she kept it trained on me.

'How did he know?' I repeated. 'And how did he know that Jason was involved?'

Ma lifted her eyes from the floor. I have never seen anyone look so wretched. 'They planned it together, didn't they?' she said. 'Doug was going to be the inside man. He was going to open the gates and the others were going to tie him up. So the police wouldn't suspect him. But he lost his nerve and went to his boss—' She broke off, too upset to continue.

Something had struck me about her voice. A hint of Irish was coming through. It must have been the stress. And that answered another question. Ma Drury was Doreen, Doreen was Ma Drury. It wouldn't have been difficult to turn the accent up when she needed to.

The hand holding the gun was shaking. Ma used her other hand to steady it, but her finger was still curled round the trigger. Worried that the last seconds of my life were running out, I tried to keep the conversation going. 'So when you found out that Doug had informed on your son,' I said, 'you got Brian Loughty—'

'You've got it wrong, Mr Quirke,' she said. 'Brian didn't kill Hamilton – I did. He went down on his knees and begged me for his life. But why should I listen? He didn't set much store on Jason's, did he?'

She squinted along the sights. 'Move away from me. Get back against the wall.'

I did as she said. The moment my shoulder blades touched it, everything vanished in a white flash. I felt myself flying through the air, then falling, slowly, like a piece of ash drifting back to earth after a fire.

32

I was lucky. Ma's bullet went into my shoulder instead of my heart. There wasn't any pain, not then, because I knocked myself out on the concrete floor when I fell. The bullet missed the arteries, the doctors told me, but I still bled buckets. I would have bled to death if a young man hadn't come to Drury Properties in search of accommodation. He was standing at the front door looking at the *Closed* sign when he heard two gunshots. He called the police and I ended up in A&E.

There were two shots because Ma turned the gun on herself after she put a bullet through my shoulder. I'm glad I didn't see that. She stuck the barrel in her mouth and pulled the trigger. As she'd said, it was impossible for her to go on.

I came round as they were putting me into the ambulance. That's when the pain hit. By the time we reached the hospital, my shoulder had swollen to the size of a football. I fainted when they lifted me on the trolley and came round when somebody fitted a mask over my face. Then I was taken down for surgery. When I came out of the anaesthetic, I was moved to the High Dependency Unit.

'I don't believe it,' Phil said. It was the following evening. He'd cut short his trip to New York and flown back when he heard the news.

'Keep your voice down,' I said.

He looked round the crowded unit and spoke more quietly. 'I want an explanation. And it had better be a good one.'

'It started with the robbery at Fearings,' I told him. 'Jason Drury knew that Doug worked there as a security guard. His mother must have told him – there wasn't much Ma didn't know about her tenants. At some stage, he and Doug worked out a plan to rob them.'

Phil screwed up his face. 'What? Doug rob his boss? That's worse than dealing drugs from the security hut.'

'Don't forget that Doug and Conrad were hard up,' I said. 'The plan was for Doug to open the gates, then Jason and his mate would overpower him so that it wouldn't look like an inside job. But Doug must have got cold feet. He told his employers, they informed the police and the police set a trap. The robbery went ahead as planned. Doug unlocked the gates and Jason and his mate tied him up. Then they locked him in a shed. They didn't know there were vanloads of police waiting round the back of Fearing's. They were caught in the act.'

'How long did Jason get?' Phil said.

'Eighteen years. The police found a shotgun in his van, so they charged him with armed robbery.'

'And Doug?'

'Fearings gave him a handsome cash reward. That's why he was in the money. He didn't get it from selling paintings, and he didn't get it from selling drugs.'

Phil poured himself a glass of water from my bedside cabinet. 'I still don't understand,' he said. 'Where does Ma Drury come in?'

'She knew it must have been Doug who shopped her son. So she decided to make him pay for it.'

Phil was looking at me with something approaching admiration. 'That's a fine piece of detective work,' he said. 'I'd like to know how you figured it out.'

'The robbery was the key,' I told him. 'I couldn't understand why Doug didn't get into trouble for opening the gates. Don't you think it odd that he didn't get the sack, even though what he did was against company rules? That didn't seem right to his workmates, and the more I thought about it, the less it seemed right to me.

'But as soon as I learned that Jason Drury was one of the robbers, everything fell into place. I knew that someone had tipped off the police because they were lying in wait. The only question was who tipped them off. I thought immediately of Doug, because he hadn't got into trouble for opening the gates.'

'And he'd come into all that money,' said Phil.

'Exactly. The next question was who would have wanted to kill him. That was easy. I knew how Ma felt about the hard time Jason was having in prison. The Drurys have never been the sort to forgive and forget.'

I was waiting for Phil to say he could have solved it himself if he hadn't been out of the country, but he was rubbing his chin thoughtfully. 'There's a lot you haven't explained,' he said. 'Why would Vilday send a couple of men to beat you up if he had nothing to do with Doug Hamilton's murder?'

'He didn't send them. Ma did. They were working for her.'

'I'm a fool, then,' Phil said. 'But how did you figure that out?'

'When I followed up what Miss Prim told me about Arthur Drury,' I said, 'I discovered that he'd done time with a criminal called Brian Loughty. They'd shared a cell in Belmarsh Prison. Later, I learned that the man who ambushed me in Tooth Lane was also called Brian Loughty. There couldn't have been two psychopaths with that name. He and Arthur went back a long way, so I guess Ma felt she could ask him a favour.'

'And when she heard you were looking for Doug's killer—'

'She sent him after me.'

Phil thought it over. 'I never met Ma Drury, but from what you told me she was a kindly old stick.'

'At first I thought she'd got Loughty to kill Doug,' I said. 'But she told me she'd done it herself.'

'I would never have thought her capable.'

'You didn't hear her screaming and shouting about how they were treating Jason in prison.'

'So we've got our story,' Phil said. 'If only you hadn't been taken in by that Nudds woman, we'd have got it a lot sooner.'

'Wait a minute,' I said, 'who's *we*?'

Phil laughed. 'What have you told the police?'

'Nothing,' I said. 'They turned up this morning and asked why Mrs Drury would want to shoot me. I said I had no idea. Then they asked why she'd want to shoot herself. Search me, I said. What were you doing in her office? they asked. I told them I went to get my deposit back after ending my tenancy. I had the tenancy agreement to prove it.'

'So they don't know that Ma killed Doug?'

'No one knows,' I said. 'That's why I told you to keep your voice down.'

Phil has rarely looked so pleased. 'Echo Press are bound to publish us now,' he said. 'We'll have to change a few names, of course, but not the murderer's. It'll be a sensation when it comes out.'

33

My holiday, if I could call it that, was over, so I turned my mind to new challenges. As soon as I was discharged from hospital, I wrote to Mr Connor in Hadgate House to tell him I now knew the identity of Doug's murderer. I promised I would report everything to Conrad's legal team, and ask them to apply to the Court of Appeal for the conviction to be quashed. It would take time, I warned, and there was no guarantee that the appeal would succeed. But I was sure my letter would set Mr Connor's mind at rest. He would know that his son was innocent. And that the criminal justice system had made another terrible mistake.

Weeks slipped by and I heard nothing back. I was beginning to wonder if something had happened to him, then one day a large package arrived from Exeter. It contained a painting in a plastic frame. Judging by the style, it was the work of a beginner. I looked for the artist's signature and found *C. Connor* in a corner. Measuring about fourteen by eighteen inches, the painting showed two men standing outside a property on what looked like a housing estate. Beside them, propped against the front wall, a shiny extension ladder reached to the eaves. In the men's hands were buckets and mysterious yellow blobs, which I took to represent squeegees or chamois cloths. It was only then that I realised the house must have been where the Connor family had lived in Tilbury, the one from which Mr Connor ran his window cleaning business. The two men were Conrad and his father. It was a summer's day, represented by a bright blue sky and crudely-painted sunbeams which radiated across the entire canvas. Father and son were grinning broadly and looking confidently out. 'I have a bright future,' the expression on Conrad's face said. It was a picture of a young man with everything to live for.

Thank you for all you have done for Conrad, Mr Connor had written in a shaky but well-formed hand on the accompanying note. *Please accept this token of our appreciation. You were the only friend who stood beside Conrad from first to last. From the bottom of our hearts, Nora and I will always be grateful for the faith you showed in him.*

The compliment made me uneasy. When the jury retired to begin its deliberations, I was far from convinced that Conrad was innocent. My not guilty vote did nothing more than register my belief that a conviction would be unsafe. To my mind, the prosecution had not proved their case beyond reasonable doubt. And the anger I'd felt in the jury room was not because I believed we were convicting an innocent man. It was because my fellow jurors weren't following the judge's instructions. Evaluate every piece of evidence, she'd told us, before you decide on your verdict.

At that time, I knew nothing about the embryonic movement to reform the English jury system that was gathering strength in legal circles. I believed that I was the only person to have misgivings about the way juries conduct their business. But long after I'd returned to work at Williams Wells, an article in a Sunday newspaper caught my eye. It described how a professor of law at one of our universities was canvassing legal professionals about the need for reform. The article mentioned an earlier campaign the professor had conducted, one that called for a more extensive vetting of jurors. It had also called for foremen and women to be trained in how to chair meetings, and for juries to present the reasons for their decisions in open court. Feeling the need to get in touch with this professor, I contacted her at her university.

She agreed to meet me for lunch and we settled on a pub not far from the British Museum. I arrived early and waited for her in the busy street outside. Bang on time, the professor came striding along the pavement, a heavy briefcase in her hand. She was tall and athletic, the sort of woman who runs the London Marathon for charity while holding down a top job and raising a growing family at the same time.

Although her previous attempt to bring about reform had failed, she told me, there was no way she was going to give up. She listened to my account of the jury's behaviour in the Connor case and took careful notes. What I said didn't seem to surprise her – she must have heard it many times before – but she assured me that it would help her new campaign. We parted friends, feeling the ties of a common purpose, one to which I hoped I had made a contribution, no matter how small.

Getting the book deal back was a cause for celebration. The advance we received from Echo Press enabled me to hire a lawyer to fight my divorce case, and it more than repaid Phil for the money he'd sunk into our investigation. My career got a new lease of life, too. While I'd been away, Williams Wells had decided to install a state-of-the-art direct dialling system. Built round an artificial intelligence program, it was powerful enough to trace debtors to every corner of the globe. That would mean a massive expansion of business, so I decided to stay with the company. I found myself a flat to rent in Chiswick and started getting to know my new neighbours. As for Riverwell, I promised myself I would never go back. Now that I lived in the world of flower festivals and poetry readings at the library, I had no desire to return to the world of revenge killings and witness intimidation.

I can't claim it was easy to put the past behind me. If a programme came on TV about advances in forensic science, I'd change channel. A press photo of a police frogman emerging from a river with something in his hands could ruin my day, even though I knew he was two hundred miles from Putney. I couldn't even bring myself to watch Phil's crime series when it was aired. I had to keep reminding myself that only two people knew what had happened in Tooth Lane – Phil, whose loyalty was beyond question, and someone else who'd done me the service of silencing herself for ever. Time passed, I got a grip on my nerves, my sleep improved, and I concentrated on getting on with my life.

Of Blanche and Kiff I heard no more. I hadn't expected to – Kiff was in prison for possessing an unlicensed firearm, and I did not regard Blanche as a threat. Until one afternoon I switched on the TV to watch a rugby match. An arts programme was winding up by interviewing an actor about the roles he'd played.

'The movie did well,' the actor was saying.

'It did hugely well,' the interviewer agreed, then we were back to the anchor, a young woman in a shiny trouser suit. Instead of signing off, she raised her hand to her ear as a message scrolled across the bottom of the screen.

BREAKING NEWS – Gangland execution in Essex

'Before the next programme, we're going over to Little Nessing in Essex,' she announced. The picture switched to a red-roofed church in a pretty village. Farmland stretched all around, as far as the eye could see. The flat Essex countryside was so familiar that I felt a tug of nostalgia. Zooming in, the camera showed yards of fluttering police tape and figures in scene of crime suits. Police vans were parked on the grassy verge in front of the church.

'Police have revealed that a body has been found buried in a field behind St Giles' Church in Little Nessing,' the on-the-scene reporter said. 'The victim, a man in his forties, was discovered in a shallow grave. He was lying face down with his hands tied behind his back. Police are saying that he had been shot in the back of the head—'

He had been discovered by a man walking his dog. Or more precisely, discovered by the dog, who'd started pawing the ground and couldn't be called away. The walker had gone back to find out what was so interesting, and called the police when he realised what his dog was digging up.

'It was sheer chance that the body was found,' the reporter said. The screen showed a wide-angle view of the field, then switched to a close-up of a police superintendent standing in front of a hedge.

'The deceased was known as a criminal,' the superintendent told viewers in a flat, emotionless voice. 'Lines of enquiry are taking place with that in mind. He may have been involved in some form of drug-related activity, and we believe that this may have been a gangland execution. The dead man has been identified as Gregory Emmanuel Vilday—'

Thoughts of rugby vanished and my mind went back to where it had all started. Blanche running after me in the street, her blonde hair tangling across her face, her desperate cries of 'Sir – sir – .' Her hatred for the man who had raped her sister. The fear that crossed her face when I pulled the PK-32 out of my pocket in her sitting room. She couldn't have known I had no intention of using it. For all the trouble she had caused me, there was something special about her, and that had kept my finger off the trigger. Maybe it was a hint of the innocence she must once have possessed, an innocence that others had taken from her.

I almost felt sorry for Vilday. It wasn't a nice way to go. But he had a debt to pay, and Blanche had collected where the criminal justice system had failed. I don't know how she managed to pull it off, but the details don't matter. I'm sure that no one will trace the killing back to her.

This book is printed on paper from sustainable sources managed under the Forest Stewardship Council (FSC) scheme.

It has been printed in the UK to reduce transportation miles and their impact upon the environment.

For every new title that Troubador publishes, we plant a tree to offset CO_2, partnering with the More Trees scheme.

For more about how Troubador offsets its environmental impact, see www.troubador.co.uk/about/